O.
A
DARK
SEA

A DCI Dani Bevan novel

By

KATHERINE
PATHAK

Edited by: The Currie Revisionists, 2015

≈

THE GARANSAY PRESS

The DCI Dani Bevan novels:

Against A Dark Sky

On A Dark Sea

The Imogen and Hugh Croft Mysteries:

Aoife's Chariot

The Only Survivor

Lawful Death

The Woman Who Vanished

Memorial For The Dead

The Garansay Press, 2015

Prologue

The fishing trawler should only have been carrying ten passengers. It wasn't insured for any more. This technical detail, however, was the last thing on the mind of the boat's captain right at this moment.

His vessel was being tossed to and fro by the waves. Its skipper fought hard to keep the heavy wheel under control. He was using only one of the ship's powerful headlamps due to the fact their voyage was less than legit. It was almost impossible for him to see what lay in the dark waters ahead.

Down below, a group of men and women sat close together in a cramped space which stank of fish and diesel in equal, sickening measure. One of the younger girls scrambled to her feet. Moving with determination, she climbed the slippery ladder and leapt onto the deck. She stumbled to the side of the boat and proceeded to retch her guts up into the foaming spray.

When her stomach was finally purged, she wiped her mouth with the back of her hand and surveyed the scene. There was blackness all around them, except for a tiny beam being projected from the bow of the boat. It was illuminating the towering waves. The girl could also make out the occasional zig-zag of moonlight attempting to cut through the thick cloud. She felt her nausea rise once again at the sight of the churning sea. Despite the terrifying conditions, she was still relieved to be up top, breathing in the cold, sharp air.

'I told you to stay in the cabin!' The angry words

4

were carried towards her on the wind.

She didn't reply, but hugged her arms tightly around her thin body and stared out into the night.

The moonlight was suddenly extinguished. It took the girl a few seconds to work out the reason why. But then she saw it. A wall of water, maybe thirty feet high was rushing towards the boat, engulfing everything in its path. By the time she'd registered the danger, it was already upon them.

The deafening roar of the wave crashing down onto the vessel almost instantly gave way to an eerie silence. The moon lit up the sea once again. This time, no man-made objects broke the rolling surface. The little fishing boat was nowhere to be seen.

*

Chapter One

The Pitt Street Headquarters of Police Scotland, Glasgow.

'It's not like Phil to be late,' DCI Dani Bevan muttered to herself, as she gazed out of her office window at the Detective Sergeant's empty workstation. It was half past nine. For Phil Boag, this was the equivalent of midday. The guy was usually in before seven am.

Dani delved into the top drawer of her filing cabinet, looking for a hand mirror to check her make-up. She had a meeting with the Chief Superintendent in five minutes. Her team were working on an anti-terrorist operation which involved sifting through hundreds of hours of online correspondence. She'd been relying on Phil to provide her with the latest analysis. Now Dani would be going in to see Nicholson empty handed. The prospect made her distinctly nervous.

DCS Angus Nicholson sat behind a huge, shiny desk. The room was completely devoid of evidence that any work took place in it. Plenty of other senior officers at the station surrounded themselves with files and papers, but not Angus.

'What's the latest on the Gallowgate Cell?'

'We've worked through all of the phone material, Sir. Now Sergeant Boag has started on their social media interactions. So far, there's nothing to indicate a conspiracy to harm.' Dani hoped this was true. She'd not actually spoken to Phil yet.

'I see. You've filed for a great deal of overtime on this case. What's your instinct, Danielle? Is it worth pursuing any further?' Nicholson steepled his hands, peering expectantly at her, obviously hoping she would give him the green light to close the operation down.

Before she had time to answer, Dani's bleeper went off. 'Sorry Sir, I'd better respond to this.'

Nicholson gestured towards the telephone on his desk, appearing rather put out by the DCI's insistence that she stick to the basic rules of policing. Dani picked up the receiver and dialled. She listened for a few moments and replaced it gently.

'Something's come up, Sir.'

'Is it serious?'

'It might be. A girl from Jane Boag's school has gone missing.'

Nicholson sat up straighter in his seat. 'Have the press got hold of it?'

'I'm not sure.'

'Then get on the case immediately, Bevan. We need this cleared up before we're hit by a media storm.'

'Right you are, Sir,' Dani carefully replied, turning on her heels and striding purposefully out of the door.

*

It was wet as DCI Bevan and DC Andy Calder climbed out of the car. They proceeded towards the entrance of Newton High School and were escorted straight to Jane Boag's office on the ground floor of the main building.

As they entered, Jane was sitting behind her desk and DS Phil Boag was standing by the window. Another woman was seated in the chair opposite the

Headmistress. She was slumped over uncomfortably, gripping a mug of tea with both hands.

DS Boag stepped forward. 'Mrs Riddell, this is DCI Danielle Bevan. She's here to help us find Maisie.'

Fiona Riddell turned around, her expression pained. She immediately stood up. Getting the opportunity to look at her properly, Dani placed the woman in her late forties. Her hair was dark brown and shoulder-length. She was slim and smartly dressed. On any normal day, Fiona would be rather attractive. 'I called the police last night. They told me to wait until morning. I haven't slept at all. As soon as dawn broke I decided to ring Phil and Jane. I thought they'd know what to do.'

'Please sit down, Mrs Riddell,' Dani urged.

The DCI already knew something of the backstory. Maisie Riddell was good friends with Phil's youngest daughter, Georgina. They were in some of the same classes together at the High School where Jane Boag was the Headmistress. 'Could you tell me the last time you had any contact with Maisie?'

Fiona was perched on the edge of the seat, her hands clasped together. 'It was yesterday morning, as she set out for school. We only live a ten minute walk away. Maisie usually meets Georgina at the gate and they go into class together.'

Dani glanced towards Mrs Boag.

'Maisie was registered during Form Time. She attended her lessons until lunch. Then she was timetabled for an activity in the Gym. But there is some uncertainty over whether or not she actually participated.' Jane appeared uncomfortable. Dani imagined that a member of staff must have been lax with their registering of the group. It wouldn't normally matter too much. Only in circumstances like this.

'We'll need to speak with her classmates and the relevant teachers in order to clarify that,' Detective Constable Andy Calder put in.

'She just didn't come home,' Fiona continued. 'I waited until six and then started to call around her friends. None of them had seen her. That's when I rang the police. They told me there was nothing they could do at such an early stage. Maisie is fourteen years old and they seemed to assume she was out in town with a boyfriend.'

'And you've received no messages from her since?' Dani asked gently.

The woman shook her head.

Phil Boag pulled out a chair and sat next to Fiona. 'Does Maisie have a boyfriend?'

She looked at him. 'No. I don't think so. Maisie doesn't go out without me knowing where she is and who she's with, just like Georgina.'

Phil placed his hand on her arm. 'What about Charles? Have you tried to contact him to see if he's heard from your daughter?'

Dani shot her Sergeant an enquiring glance.

'Maisie's father,' he mouthed back to her.

'Not yet. He'll only get angry. It won't help.'

'I'm afraid we will need to get in touch with your ex-husband, Mrs Riddell. I'd like you to provide us with his full name and address, including his work number if possible.'

Fiona nodded and scrabbled around in her handbag. 'You'd be better off ringing him at work. He's there most of the time. Charles is an executive at Barents Oil, based at their head offices in Stavanger.'

'Norway?' Dani asked in surprise.

'Yes, Maisie's father has lived there for the past five years.' The woman finally dug out a dog-eared business card and handed it to the DCI.

'Thank you. If you've finished your tea, Mrs Riddell, DC Calder and I will escort you home. We'd like to take a look at Maisie's bedroom and it will be more comfortable for us to talk there.'

Dani signalled to Phil and they both helped Maisie's mother out of her chair. They had to support her weight between them on the short walk to the car-park. Dani wasn't sure she was fit to drive, but Fiona assured them she was. Bevan and Calder followed close behind in the squad car, weaving slowly through the suburban streets of the south side of Glasgow, just in case it turned out the poor woman was not.

Chapter Two

'Sorry I didn't let you know what was going on earlier, Ma'am. Fiona Riddell was in a terrible state when she arrived on our doorstep at the crack of dawn. I wanted to get all the information I could out of her then and there,' Phil Boag declared, as Bevan and Calder returned to the Pitt Street station.

'No problem. It's not like you to be late. I knew something serious must be up.' Dani deposited her rain jacket on a stand and signalled for the two men to join her in the office. She pulled the door closed behind them.

Directing her comments to Phil, Dani said, 'when we searched Maisie's room, it became clear that she'd taken some clothes from out of her wardrobe, a few items of underwear and a soft bag. Fiona Riddell hadn't noticed this earlier on as she hadn't thought to check. Do you think the girl may have done a bunk? How well did Maisie get on with her mother?'

Phil ran a hand through his silver-streaked hair. 'Fine, I think. Georgina certainly never mentioned them having rows. Although, I'm not sure how much she would share with me and Jane. To be honest, I'm really surprised to hear that Maisie might have taken off.' Boag crinkled his handsome face in concentration. He was tall and lean, with a muscular upper body. Dani knew that Jane Boag's career took priority in their household. It didn't mean Phil wasn't dedicated to his job. He just had no desire to move up through the ranks.

'Would you mind if we questioned Georgina? You or Jane can be present, of course. I'm going over to the High School to conduct the interviews, once we've finished here,' Andy Calder said cautiously.

Phil nodded. 'Sure. I think it might be better to have Jane there. Georgie has a thing about the other kids knowing I'm a policeman. It's bad enough her being the child of the Headmistress.' Phil gave a rueful smile.

'I understand,' Andy swiftly added. 'I'll tread very carefully.'

When Calder had left the room, Dani turned to Phil. 'We've got an all-ports warning out on Maisie. She hasn't got a passport with her, so the girl can't have got far.'

'Are we certain this isn't a case of abduction?'

Dani glanced down at the school photograph on her desk. A pretty, pale-faced girl with straight black hair and emerald green eyes stared back at her. The smile that danced upon her lips looked contrived for the occasion. 'Maisie's parents divorced five years ago, is that right?'

Phil took a seat. 'Yes, Maisie Riddell was still in primary school when her father moved to Norway. The family had been living in Aberdeen before that. After Charles Riddell was off the scene, Fiona had no reason to stay on in the city. She moved back to Glasgow, where she had grown up. The girls hit it off as soon as Maisie joined the same class. She and Georgie have been great pals ever since.'

'How did Maisie take her parents' separation? It must have been particularly tough when her father moved out of the country.'

'From what Fiona has told us, Charles worked very long hours. When he was offered a major job at Barents Oil, Fiona refused to go with him. The marriage was already rocky and she didn't fancy being stuck in Stavanger on her own. But I've never heard Maisie speak about it. Her dad comes over every few months and she spends alternate Christmases with them.'

'Them?' Dani enquired.

'Yes, Charles re-married a couple of years back. They've now got a toddler. A wee boy, I believe.'

Dani looked thoughtful. 'I asked Jim Caffrey to examine what was on the camera outside the school. It seems that Maisie left the premises just after lunch. She definitely bunked afternoon Games. The footage shows her leaving through the gates alone and carrying two bags. I'm waiting to get the CCTV discs from Queen Street and Central Stations, plus the bus depots. Maisie's certainly headed somewhere of her own accord. We just need to find out where, before she gets herself wound up in the wrong type of company.'

Phil nodded, appearing deeply troubled by her words. Dani could tell he was thinking about his own daughters and picturing them in a similar scenario.

'We never quite know what's going on in their heads, do we?' Dani offered.

'No,' he said distractedly, 'we don't.'

*

DC Andy Calder had arranged to interview Maisie Riddell's friends and classmates in the department of the school welfare officer, who had agreed to be present throughout. Andy was relieved that she was there. He knew this was going to be a sensitive case. Jane Boag was a high profile figure in Glasgow. She was a member of several government committees on education and had a hotline to the First Minister. Phil was an easy-going kind of guy who Andy had worked with for years. His wife, on the other hand, was an entirely different proposition.

The welfare officer, Katie Law, had pulled a couple of brightly coloured sofas into the centre of the space and brought in a tray of tea, coffee and biscuits. Andy was grateful for her mumsy presence beside him as the first of the students entered the room. It was Georgina Boag. Her mother had wisely decided to let them interview her alone. Andy hoped he'd get more out of her this way. The girl was small and fair-haired. She immediately struck him as young for her years.

'No thank you, Mrs Law,' Georgie said quietly, after the woman had offered her a drink.

'Do you remember me, Georgina? I work with your father. We met at his fortieth birthday party, although that was a wee while back now,' Andy began.

She nodded and smiled. 'I remember. You were the one who had a baby. Dad showed us the photos.'

'Well, it was Carol who did the difficult bit, but I have got a little girl, that's right.' Andy shuffled forward. 'Can you tell me when you last saw Maisie?'

Georgina gazed down at her lap. 'In French class, yesterday morning. Maisie didn't come to lunch. She said she had something to do in town.'

'Are you allowed to leave the school premises during the day?' Andy glanced at Katie Law, who shook her head.

'No,' Georgina answered. 'But Maisie occasionally did. It isn't too difficult. The gates are open for deliveries and stuff most of the time.'

'I see. Did she tell you where she was going?'

'Not really. She just used to get a bus into the city centre, look around the shops and that kind of thing.'

'It must have been difficult for her to have the

time to do that. Maisie would need to be back for her afternoon lessons, wouldn't she?'

'Aye, but she only went into town on the days we had activities after lunch. Mr Kirk never takes a register. He hasn't got a clue who we are.'

Katie Law frowned and made a note in her file.

'So this was a regular arrangement? Did you ever go with her, Georgina? You won't get into trouble if you did. We just want to get Maisie home safely. If we know where she usually went to during the day, it could be a huge help to us.'

Georgina looked directly at Calder. Her large eyes were glistening. 'I only wish I had. Then, I might have an idea of where she's gone. But I never had the guts. Mum would make my life a misery if she found out I'd played truant from her precious school. It would make the front page of the Record.'

Andy suspected this wasn't an exaggeration and it might very well have done. 'How did Maisie get on with her mum?'

Georgina shrugged. 'Okay. Mrs Riddell lets Maisie do loads more things than my parents. She can watch 18 certificate films and one time she got the plane to her dad's all by herself.'

Andy lifted his head from his notes. 'How long ago was that?'

'About three months. She went to Norway for Christmas. Her mum put her on the plane at Glasgow Airport and her dad met her at the other end. Maisie said it looks magical there in winter, with all the snow and the fir trees.'

Andy was aware that many parents allowed their children to travel unaccompanied on aeroplanes. The stewards usually watched out for them during the flight. Nonetheless, it suggested something to him about the amount of freedom the girl was given. 'You've known Maisie for a long time. Could she have run away from home?'

Proper tears escaped onto Georgina's cheeks. 'I don't think so, we were always really happy. She and I had a good laugh together, we shared everything. I don't understand why she'd go away and leave me alone. I thought she was my friend.'

Katie Law leant across and placed an arm around the girl's shoulders. She snuggled into the woman's comfortable embrace.

'That's all for now, Georgina, you've been really helpful.' Andy smiled as the girl got up to leave, thinking it strange that in the minds of teenagers, the universe revolved entirely around themselves.

Chapter Three

DCI Bevan's ground floor flat was in the Scotstounhill area of north-west Glasgow. She kicked her court shoes off in the wide hallway and padded into the kitchen-diner at the rear of the property without switching on the lights. Dani sat at the solid wood table and gazed out into her small but secluded garden.

It was mid-March and spring buds were attempting to break through the barren and spiky vegetation that currently dominated her plot. Despite this sign that winter was finally over, the temperature remained low. Dani hoped that wherever she was, Maisie Riddell had access to shelter and food.

The detective forced herself to get up, flick on the spotlights and enter the kitchen area. Dani prepared a simple meal which she ate at the breakfast bar separating the two halves of the room.

Since the discovery that Maisie had packed a bag to take with her, Phil found out the girl had emptied her savings account three days previously. Andy Calder and two other members of the team were in the process of trawling through Maisie's computer history, to see if there was a chance the girl was planning to abscond with somebody she'd met online. So far, there was no evidence of this. Maisie had barely used any of the usual social media sites.

Andy Calder's interviews with Maisie's classmates didn't throw up any obvious leads either. It seemed as if Georgie Boag was the girl's only really close friend. Dani assumed that as Georgie was the headmistress's daughter, Maisie hadn't thought it prudent to share her plans with her. Bevan was now waiting for the CCTV footage from the St Enoch Centre and Buchanan Street to arrive so they could try and identify what Maisie Riddell did in town during the Wednesday afternoons that she played truant from Newton High School. Dani suspected this information would prove to be the key to the investigation.

Bevan placed her empty plate in the dishwasher. She intended to do nothing else except collapse into bed. It was very difficult during the case of a missing child to switch your thoughts off at the end of the day. But she had to. An exhausted officer leading the inquiries would do nothing to help Fiona or Maisie Riddell. Nonetheless, the grainy image of the young girl's face, with its mixture of anticipation and fear, caught on camera outside the school gate yesterday lunchtime, was still burned into her brain when she finally closed her eyes.

The following morning, Dani noticed the red light flickering on her answering machine. She furrowed her brow, thinking she must have slept so soundly that she'd never heard the phone in the hallway ringing last evening. Bevan pressed the button. The detective smiled at the sound of Bill Hutchison's voice. Dani had met Bill and his wife on her last case and they became good friends. The couple very sadly lost their son in the same year that Dani's mother had died. This shared grief seemed to have created a kind of bond between them.

Once Bill had given a brief account of what he and Joy had been up to during a weekend they'd spent with their grandchildren, the man's tone became more serious. He asked if she'd had chance yet to look into the case of a murdered fisherman in Stonehaven. Dani shook her head with frustration and strode into the kitchen to make breakfast, allowing Bill's voice to fade into background noise. She really didn't need any extra burdens being added to her already massive workload. Dani wanted her mind to be focussed solely on young Maisie. She owed the girl that much at least.

But as Bevan drove her little hatchback towards the Pitt Street station, she couldn't prevent her thoughts from straying to the words that Bill had spoken during their last encounter. He was convinced that the murder of a middle aged man in a boat shed in Stonehaven was the work of Richard Erskine, the person that Dani had brought to court on a multiple murder charge a few months ago and was acquitted. The guy had been clearly guilty, the forensic evidence was unequivocal, but the jury had somehow felt sympathy for him. Erskine claimed he'd killed only to protect his beloved grandmother's secret, a woman who'd suffered the most terrible abuse as a child and had stabbed to death the man responsible.

The Stonehaven murder appeared to match the fate of the last of Erskine's victims in every detail. Both men were found in worksheds, their throats brutally cut and their bodies positioned carefully after death so that their hands lay palm up in their laps. Bill believed that Erskine had struck again, although there was no other obvious connection between him and the dead fisherman. Bevan had already alerted the senior investigating officer to the similarities in the two cases. She didn't have the jurisdiction to interfere any further.

Dani banished all thoughts of the Stonehaven case from her mind as she stepped out of the lift into the open-plan work area of the Serious Crime Unit.

Bevan immediately called her officers over for a briefing. On a series of display boards and flip charts were arranged stills from the CCTV footage of Maisie Riddell at the gates of the school. Various photographs of the girl and her parents were pinned up around them. A timeline had been created of Maisie's movements in the 24 hours leading up to her disappearance.

DC Andy Calder was the first to provide his input. 'We did find some footage of Maisie Riddell at the St Enoch Centre last Wednesday, Ma'am, but there was no sign of her yesterday. It seems she was doing exactly what Georgina Boag claimed. The girl was looking around the shops. At one stage, she bought a burger and fries. She sat on one of the benches by the escalator to eat it.'

'Did she meet or talk to anyone else that you could see?' Dani enquired.

Andy shook his head. 'But one thing did strike us. The girl wasn't just window shopping. In the last of the images she appeared in, Maisie had a couple of carrier bags. They were from boutique shops rather than the big chains.'

'So the stuff she'd bought wasn't cheap,' Dani supplied. 'How much money did Maisie withdraw from her bank account, Phil?'

'A couple of thousand, Ma'am.'

A few whistles went up.

'But Fiona told me that was all the savings she and her husband had put aside for their daughter over the years. When you think of it that way, it wasn't really such a large amount. The bank told me that Charlie Riddell deposited fifty or a hundred pounds into Maisie's account every so often but the girl herself had never accessed the money before this week.'

'So if she had cash to buy clothing from

boutiques in town, where was she keeping it?' Dani glanced around the room. 'And where was it coming from?'

'Her mother says she didn't have a part-time job,' added DC Alice Mann. 'Apparently, Maisie's father didn't like the idea of it. He wanted his daughter to focus on her studies.'

'Maybe Charlie gave her money when she came to stay with him. He might have preferred to give cash to Maisie directly, rather than having to clear it with Fiona,' Phil put in.

'Well, we can ask him when he arrives later on today. Charlie Riddell's flight is due to land at six. He's staying at the Hotel Ecosse in Hillhead.' Dani looked thoughtful. She ran a hand through her short, dark hair. 'Maisie must have been feeling put out by her father's new marriage and particularly by the arrival of a baby.'

'If she was then the girl never showed it,' Phil said decisively. 'I spoke with Georgie again last night. She maintains that Maisie was perfectly contented and had no reason to be disaffected at home.'

Dani turned to look at one of the photographs. To the DCI, Maisie's watery-green eyes seemed to contain a terrible sadness. 'Then the girl must have been confiding her feelings to somebody else. It doesn't appear to have been anyone she hooked up with online, so we need to find out exactly where Maisie could have contacted this person or persons.' She twisted back to address the group. 'Because if there's one thing I'm certain of, it's that Maisie Riddell did not organise this little flit alone.'

Chapter Four

Bevan was seated to the left of Charles Riddell. His ex-wife was on his right. The man appeared slightly dishevelled, especially compared to the women he was positioned between, both of whom had dressed carefully for this occasion.

When a couple of minutes were given over for photographs, at the very start of the press conference, Maisie's father flinched at the sudden assault of flashes, putting a hand up to shield his eyes. Dani wondered if he'd been drinking on the plane. It wasn't a gesture she would have recommended he make. The man was going to look guilty and defensive on the front cover of every national newspaper the next morning.

Bevan gave a succinct outline of the case before handing over to Fiona and Charles to present their appeal. She never coached a victim's family before a press briefing. Their words had to appear natural and unforced. The British public could be a fickle bunch. Even if you'd lost a loved one in the most appalling circumstances, they weren't averse to condemning you for the way you were handling it.

The Riddells did the job extremely well. Fiona was measured and calm, but very obviously devastated. Charles was clearly upset too, but he said all the right things. They both appealed directly to Maisie, promising to fix everything if she'd just come home. There wasn't any animosity evident between the couple. When the journalists had piled out, Dani led them up to her office and ordered tea. She pulled the door closed gently.

'Thank you for doing that Mr and Mrs Riddell. I know it isn't easy, but the publicity a press conference generates can really help.' Dani sat on a soft seat opposite the pair, who had taken the little sofa. The detective didn't want there to be a desk between them.

'Has anyone reported seeing Maisie since yesterday? *Someone* must have spotted her.' Charles looked desperate. He was a handsome and well-built man in his late forties. His hair was thick and grey but his face remained surprisingly unlined.

'It's very early days, Mr Riddell. This evening's appeal will certainly help. We have viewed a great deal of CCTV footage but Maisie does not seem to have left the city via the train or bus stations.'

'But I thought the first 24 hours were crucial? How can it possibly be early days?' Charles shifted about in his seat.

'That is in the case of an abduction. The evidence does not suggest this is what happened to Maisie,' Dani said kindly, silently cursing the inaccuracies of police procedure pedalled by television dramas.

'The detectives are convinced that Maisie ran away,' Fiona explained flatly. 'She'd packed a bag and emptied her bank account.'

Charles rubbed at his stubbly chin. 'Why would she do that? Maisie was happy. She could have whatever she wanted from us. I'd never let her go without.' The man appeared utterly bemused and lost.

Dani turned to Fiona, who was wearing a smart black trouser suit and had pinned her light brown hair away from her face. 'Did you know that Maisie had been sneaking out of school on Wednesday afternoons? She'd been truanting from Games and taking the bus into town. It appears she spent her time wandering around the shopping centres.'

Before the woman had a chance to reply, Charles butted in, '*what*? How is that possible? The school is supposed to be secure during the day. Whenever I've been to the place it's locked up like Fort Knox.'

'According to one of your daughter's friends, Maisie knew the times when the gates were likely to be open. She slipped out then,' Bevan clarified.

'I didn't realise she was doing that,' Fiona said quietly. 'But in a way, I'm not surprised. Maisie did want to have more freedom. There were several classes that she didn't feel it was necessary for her to have to attend anymore. I told Maisie it would get better when she was studying the subjects she'd chosen.'

'How could you not have known she wasn't in school?' Charles demanded.

Fiona sighed. 'Maisie is nearly fifteen. She isn't the little girl she was when you left us.'

The man's face flushed red. 'I did *not* leave you. It was *your* decision to stay behind when I went to Norway.'

Fiona rolled her eyes towards the ceiling. 'And that's been your get out of jail free card for everything that's happened since. I suppose it never occurred to you not to take the job?'

Dani cleared her throat, sensing this discussion was getting them nowhere. 'Did Maisie have a group of friends outside of school who she met up with? The evidence we have gathered so far creates the impression that she didn't plan to leave home by herself.'

Fiona thought carefully about this. 'To be honest, Maisie didn't have many friends. There's the group of girls at school you've already spoken with and the boy that lives next door to us who she occasionally chats to. Apart from my sister's kids, that's about it. Maisie is a very quiet, reserved sort of girl. That is why I find the thought of her having run away so difficult to comprehend.'

'What kind of shambolic operation is Jane Boag running, that she can't keep our daughter safe during the school day?' Charles Riddell was still red in the face and beads of sweat had broken out on his brow.

'She has over a thousand students on the premises,' Fiona muttered under her breath.

Dani leant forward and poured more tea. 'Have another drink, Mr Riddell. I'll put an extra sugar lump in. It will help.'

Charles put out a shaky hand and lifted the cup to his lips. Bevan noticed that tears were trickling down his cheeks. 'I thought she'd be okay here with her mother. It wasn't an easy choice to leave Maisie, you need to understand that. If I'd known something like this would happen then of course I'd never have taken the damned job.' The man started to sob.

Dani was surprised to see Fiona immediately turn towards her ex-husband and slip her arms tightly around him, burying her face in his shoulder.

'It's not possible to guarantee they'll always be safe, Mr Riddell. All we can do now is to focus our attention on making sure that we find her.'

After seeing the couple out of the building, Dani discovered Andy Calder waiting outside her office.

'I've had a thought, Ma'am.'

Dani gestured for him to follow her inside.

'What is it?'

'Well, I know that Fiona Riddell is a good friend of Phil's and everything, but I think we still need to keep her in the frame.'

'In what sense?' Dani was intrigued.

'Mrs Riddell looked really surprised when we discovered Maisie's stuff was missing from her bedroom. But there was something about her reaction that struck me at the time as odd. I can't quite put my finger on what it was; she just didn't seem as shocked as she might be. Then I was watching her at the press conference. Maisie's dad was a mess, but Fiona was just so incredibly cool.'

Dani appeared thoughtful. 'You suspect that Fiona Riddell may have packed that bag herself and then got rid of it. To make it appear as if her daughter had run away. Maisie *was* carrying two bags in the CCTV footage of her leaving the school.'

'Yes, but we only got a good view of the rucksack. The other bag wasn't clearly visible. It could have been a plastic carrier for all we know. Fiona Riddell had the whole of last night to cover her tracks - if she did do something to harm her daughter, that is.'

'Okay.' Dani sat behind her desk. 'Can you find out what Fiona's movements were yesterday morning and afternoon?'

Andy nodded, turning to leave.

'Oh, and keep your enquiries as discreet as possible.'

'Don't worry, Ma'am. I intend to.'

Chapter Five

DC Andy Calder returned to his desk, dipping his head to acknowledge Phil Boag as he passed. Calder reached for the file they had compiled on the Riddells. He spent a few minutes reviewing the information he had on Fiona.

Mrs Riddell was the sales manager of a small electronics company based on the outskirts of Motherwell. She drove to work each day, leaving the house just after her daughter departed for the walk to school. Fiona was 45 years old and had not re-married or changed her name since the divorce from Charles. Phil said she'd always told him and Jane that she wanted to keep the same surname as Maisie. If Fiona decided to get married again in the future, she would review the decision, but she never had.

Andy lifted the telephone receiver and called the Managing Director of the company where Fiona worked. He explained that his questions were mere formalities and not an indication that his employee was under suspicion of any sort. Calder jotted down some details. He thanked the man for his time and ended the call. Andy sat back in his seat.

The Detective Constable was only working his second major case since being hospitalized for a massive heart attack a year and a half ago, at the age of just 34. Since his recuperation, Calder had changed his lifestyle completely. He'd shed two and a half stone and spent an hour each day in the gym. Calder's upper body strength had improved considerably.

Despite this new health regime, Andy was convinced that the heart attack would mean he never rose through the ranks like his contemporaries had. His boss, DCI Bevan, was a case in point. She was only two years older than him and had gained promotion quickly and seemingly with ease. Not that Andy begrudged her this success. He liked Dani a great deal and felt she was a crucial ally for him on the force. The people that Calder had begun to resent, were the self-consciously careerist coppers who knew the right things to say to the right folk and had been to the right schools and universities.

Little did Andy know that the niggling, festering bitterness he now harboured for those colleagues was very likely as damaging to his weak heart as his previous lifestyle had been. His wife, Carol, who stayed at home with their eighteen month old daughter, Amy, had noticed this subtle change in her husband's personality. She would happily have forfeited his newly toned, muscly physique to have the easy-going, unambitious Andy back. But that man appeared to be gone for good.

Fiona Riddell had been at her office until 5pm on the Wednesday that Maisie went missing. This fitted with the woman's claim that she'd returned to the house at roughly half past, ringing around her daughter's friends at six, when the girl was still not home. But there was now a slight discrepancy in the timeline they'd been given. Fiona's boss was forced to admit that Mrs Riddell had not arrived at her desk until 10am on that particular day. He said it was no big deal to him as Fiona was a well-respected manager who regularly worked over and above her expected hours of employment, only because DC Calder was asking for specific details, did her superior feel inclined to mention it.

Andy knew he had to tread carefully. The detective sifted through the file and located the Riddells' home number. The woman answered after a couple of rings.

'Mrs Riddell? It's DC Calder here.'

'Has there been any news?'

'I'm afraid not. I'm just calling to clarify some of the details from your original statement.'

'Okay.' Fiona's tone was cautious.

'I've spoken with Malcolm Lorne, who told me that you arrived at work an hour later than usual this Wednesday.' Calder let the words settle between them.

'I had to stop at the shops on the way in. There was something I needed to buy.'

'Could you tell me which shop?' Andy tried to make the request sound as casual as possible.

'Is that really necessary? Look, fine, I stopped at the industrial estate just off junction 22 of the M8. I bought a birthday present for my sister's little girl, had a coffee, and filled up with petrol. I may have some of the receipts still in my purse. The petrol payment was made by card, so it will definitely be on my bank statement.'

'Great. That should clear things up. Sorry to bother you.'

'That's okay.' Fiona hesitated for a moment before adding, 'Charlie is here at the house with me right now. We felt we should be together if Maisie tried to ring, so if you need us for anything else then you know where to find us. Please call if there's any news at all.'

'We'll certainly do that and thank you again for your cooperation, Mrs Riddell.'

*

Dani ran a hand through her dark, cropped hair. She was examining the amended timeline that Andy had just handed her.

'I've asked Alice Mann to check with Fiona's bank about the payment made at the petrol station. We should get a time confirmation from that. I think it'll be enough to explain her movements,' Calder said.

'Was it usual for Fiona to be late into work? Why did she run those errands on that particular morning?' Dani looked her colleague in the eye, knowing he had good instincts for these things.

'I got the impression it wasn't the norm, Ma'am. Her boss described Mrs Riddell as usually extremely fastidious about time-keeping, which is why he was very reluctant to mention her lateness on this occasion.'

'Well, it's probably nothing, just the sudden realisation she needed to get her niece a present. But we'll have to bear it in mind. Any behaviour that was out of the ordinary on that day can't be ignored.'

'What about the husband, Ma'am? Can we account for his whereabouts at the time Maisie disappeared?'

'Phil's been looking into Charlie Riddell's schedule. According to his enquiries, the man was at work on Wednesday until late, at the head offices of Barents Oil in Stavanger, which is where he always is.'

'The couple seem on reasonably good terms, considering they're so long divorced,' Andy mused.

'For the time being, Fiona and Charlie are united by a common cause; to find their missing daughter. If Maisie doesn't come home within the next few days and the situation starts to drag on, that's when the recriminations will begin.'

Andy nodded grimly, quite certain his boss was right.

Chapter Six

The Boags lived in a large Victorian villa in the south Glasgow suburb of Pollockshaws. Phil was clearing away the dishes after having dinner with his two teenage daughters. The ground floor rear of the property consisted of a huge open-plan kitchen-diner. The fixtures and fittings were of the highest possible specification and had been part of a massive renovation project that Phil and Jane completed the previous year.

Phil glanced up at the clock above the impressive range cooker and noted it was quarter to seven. He didn't expect his wife to be home from work for hours yet. He placed a sheet of plastic wrap over her plate of food and slotted it into the fridge. He looked over his shoulder at the girls, who were still seated at the table, both engrossed in their tablet computers.

'What do you want for pudding?' He called over cheerfully, rummaging around in the freezer section. 'How about a piece of Granny's sponge heated up with a scoop of ice-cream?' Phil wasn't expecting a reply but he knew that Georgie would probably want some and seventeen year old Sorcha certainly would not. He'd learnt long ago not to pressurize his daughters when it came to food. They were both naturally lean like their parents. There was no need for them to become self-conscious about their physiques.

Sorcha asked to be excused and Phil was left at the table with his youngest child. She ate her dessert in silence.

'How are you doing?' He rested his hand gently on her shoulder.

Georgie made a twisting motion, as if to shake him off, but her dad kept it there. 'I'm not going back to that place.' She stared resolutely at the half-eaten contents of the bowl.

'Come on, you know you've got to. It will help to be amongst your other friends, otherwise you'll have too much time to think and worry.'

Georgina glanced up. 'I haven't *got* any other friends. Everyone hates me because of Mum.' The tears began to fall down her cheeks and Phil pulled her close. She put down her spoon and pressed her face into his shoulder. 'Why did she go away, Dad? Maisie knew I couldn't handle school without her.'

'She must have had her own reasons, love. Stuff that was more important than problems at school.'

Georgina went quiet for a moment then she said, in almost a whisper, 'Maisie thought her mum had a boyfriend.'

Phil tried to mask his surprise. 'You never told us this before. Was Maisie unhappy about it?'

Georgie shrugged her shoulders. 'She only suspected. That's why I didn't tell Mr Calder when he interviewed me. Maisie said her mum was behaving differently than normal the last few months. She was sure it was because she was seeing somebody. Do you think it could have anything to do with why Maisie left?'

'I don't know, darling, but everything is important when a child goes missing. I'll have to tell my DCI about it.'

Georgie nodded, sniffing loudly. 'Okay, I don't mind. I just want my friend back.' The girl began sobbing again and Phil held her tight, gently rocking his little girl back and forth until she was calm and still.

Phil suggested that Georgina have a bath and an early night. For once, she'd not objected to the idea. When he went into Georgie's high-ceilinged room to tuck her in, Phil told his youngest that if she didn't feel up to it in the morning she could take the day off - go to her Gran and Grandad's in Newton Mearns, perhaps. But Georgie had surprised him by saying she'd be fine. She wanted things to carry on as normal. Otherwise the whole situation would feel even worse.

Phil had nodded and turned out her light, thinking this was very sensible. He knew his daughter had to get on with her life sooner rather than later. There were absolutely no guarantees that Maisie Riddell would ever be found. Phil padded down the stairs and went into the kitchen. He observed Sorcha through the double doors which led into the lounge, long-limbed and sprawled out across the sofa, commandeering the television set. Phil didn't mind. He went to one of the hand-made cabinets and poured out a small measure of Scotch, perching up at the breakfast bar to drink it.

The Detective Sergeant had long since stopped wondering what is was that his wife did during these late nights at her office. He knew it was paperwork of some kind and the answering of crucial correspondence. The long days didn't seem to bother Jane at all. She enthusiastically threw herself into the weekends that they shared as a family. But Phil found it hard to compartmentalize his life in this way. They'd had some bad news today as a family, yet she wasn't here. The fall-out from Maisie's disappearance, the police enquiries and conversations with Fiona that followed, had eaten into Jane's busy schedule. His wife would need to work even later in order to compensate.

Phil used to worry about Jane when she came home after dark. He would stay up reading a book and wouldn't really settle until he'd heard her key turning in the lock. Phil took a gulp of whisky, feeling its warmth soothe him, as he considered how in the past few months this had no longer been the case. When he fell into bed at night these days he went straight to sleep, barely giving Jane's whereabouts a second thought. It was in Phil's nature to worry about his girls, to want to keep them safe. But his wife was late home so often that to dwell on it would have turned him into a nervous wreck. So he didn't, which he knew should really concern him even more.

Phil had spent much of the day digging into the life of Charles Riddell. He too seemed utterly driven by his career. Charles had grown up in a middle class suburb of Glasgow and attended the university in the city. That was where he had met Fiona Adams. They got married in the late nineties and moved to Aberdeen when Charles got a job with a major oil and gas company there. Maisie was born a couple of years later. Phil knew from the conversations he and Jane had with Fiona that she and Charles drifted apart as his job started to consume his every waking hour.

Charles Riddell's hard work paid off and in 2009 he was offered a key position within one of Norway's main oil companies. Fiona refused to go with him. She already felt cut off from her friends and family in Glasgow. It had seemed to her like the natural moment to end their marriage. Charles re-married in 2011. His new wife was 34 years old and called Kristin. The couple had had a baby boy the previous summer.

There appeared to Phil to be no reason for Charles Riddell to be involved in the disappearance of his daughter. There was no evidence that Maisie had been in contact with her father about her plans either.

Phil was just considering pouring another wee dram when he heard the front door opening. The noise made him jump. He glanced at the clock and noted it was 9.45pm. He didn't imagine for a second it could be Jane. Perhaps it was his mum and dad, dropping by to see if Georgina was okay. Phil levered himself off the stool and paced through to the hallway to greet them.

Jane Boag was removing her long woollen coat and scarf, hanging them onto a peg. 'Hi,' she said quietly, before glancing about her. 'How is Georgie?'

Phil stepped forward and planted a kiss on his wife's lips, not mentioning his surprise at seeing her there. 'She's gone to bed. I managed to persuade her to have an early night.'

Jane looked disappointed but said, 'good. She needed to rest. Any news about Maisie yet?'

Phil shook his head. 'We can't find any evidence of her having left Glasgow by train or bus, which is pretty unusual in the case of a runaway.'

Jane sighed. 'I'm going to have to set up my computer and do some work from here darling, but I wanted to come back and be close to you all.'

Phil slipped his arm around her waist and led his wife in the direction of the kitchen. 'Well, I'm really glad you did. Sorcha is still up. She'll certainly be pleased to see you.'

Chapter Seven

The Hutchisons' house was situated in the centre of a quiet estate in Falkirk. Joy Hutchison was already in the kitchen preparing their porridge when Bill came striding in to join her.

'You've just missed DCI Bevan being interviewed on the radio. They've still not found that young girl,' Joy immediately informed her husband.

'The poor mother,' he muttered solemnly, taking a seat at the table and pouring a cup of tea from the pot.

'Oh, I don't know,' Joy said, as she stirred the oats and water vigorously. 'The woman looked fairly composed during the press conference. Perhaps she wasn't getting on very well with her daughter before the girl left. You know what teenagers can be like. Most ordinary people aren't actors. It's very difficult to appear upset about something when you're actually not bothered at all.'

Bill ruffled the morning paper. 'Some folk just don't come across well on camera. They clam up or become positively robotic. I'm sure we shouldn't read too much into it.'

Joy didn't reply. Instead, she leant down and rummaged in a cupboard, retrieving a couple of bowls and placing them on the worktop next to the stove. 'What are you planning to do today?' She suddenly asked, turning off the light as the mixture turned thick and creamy.

'I thought I might take Rita for a run to the coast. I've been promising to take her out for weeks.' Bill kept his eyes trained on the news section.

Joy spun around, with the porridge coated spatula still held in her hand. 'But I've got a hair appointment this afternoon. I won't be able to come with you.'

'That's okay, I don't mind going on my own. You have a day to yourself.'

Joy paused, thinking she could take a shopping trip into Stirling. 'Alright. But don't wander too far afield, will you? Rita does get tired easily.'

'No, of course not.' Bill shook out the broadsheet forcefully, causing a teaspoon to tinkle against his saucer. 'We'll just go far enough to catch ourselves a bit of sea air.'

Rita McCulloch lived in a large house on the corner opposite the Hutchisons' place. Bill had always found her good company. Rita gave up her little car a couple of years before, when she no longer felt confident behind the wheel. But she missed the freedom to travel that it used to provide.

Bill told Rita to dress warmly for their trip. The pensioner had a fake fur hat and scarf with her, as well as her thick sheepskin coat when he arrived to pick her up. Bill helped the older lady climb into the passenger seat.

As they manoeuvred slowly out of the estate, he enquired if she would mind them having a slightly longer drive today, as he had a hankering to travel up the east coast.

'Oh, that would be lovely,' Rita replied with sincerity. 'I'd really like to visit somewhere new.'

'Good,' Bill said with satisfaction. 'Then just sit back and enjoy the journey.'

It took them just over two hours to reach Stonehaven. Bill stopped so they could have a coffee at a service station on the A90 when they were about halfway there. Rita smiled brightly as she finally caught sight of the grey-green waters of the North Sea.

They took a stroll around the harbour. Bill made sure that his companion was wrapped up warm. Rita was particularly impressed by the unusual rocky outcrop at the headland which supported the ruins of Dunnottar Castle. Bill asked if Rita would like to visit the Stonehaven Tollbooth, which had served as an early prison for the town and now housed a museum. The lady quickly agreed, knowing it would provide some shelter from the biting north-easterly wind.

After purchasing Rita her entry ticket, he informed his neighbour that he would come back and meet her again in thirty minutes, as he had a brief errand to run. Rita nodded her head graciously, giving Bill a broad smile. 'Of course,' she said.

Bill knew exactly what he was looking for. He strode purposefully along the seafront, pausing when he reached a small boat yard. The main entrance had been sealed off with a police cordon. A number of sailing boats were moored along the shoreline here and some of the vessels were supported on wooden struts in the yard itself. There were two worksheds, one of which was also secured firmly with blue and white tape. A uniformed policeman stood guard at the entrance.

'Oh dear,' Bill announced to the constable. 'I was hoping to be able to retrieve something from my daughter's boat. Are we not permitted to enter the yard at all?'

The PC shook his head. 'Not until all the forensic tests have been completed. Is it something urgent? I could always have a word with my boss, he'll probably let me go in and get it for you.' The young man reached for his walkie-talkie.

'No, no, it's nothing to bother your superior officer about,' Bill swiftly added. 'Do you have any idea when your inquiries may be over? My daughter and her husband were planning to take their boat on a trip in a couple of days from now.'

The policeman made a face. 'I'd tell them to make alternative plans if I were you. We're a long way off solving this one.'

'The man who was murdered, he was a local, is that right?'

'Terence Sinclair. He lived in a cottage just a few streets back. He'd been working at the boat yard these past couple of years, doing odd jobs and maintenance. It couldn't have made him much of a living.'

'Have any witnesses come forward?'

'The incident happened late in the evening, on a very inclement night. Sadly, there were very few folk out and about.' The constable sighed deeply. 'None of us can really understand why anyone would want to kill Terry Sinclair. The man was a loner, had very little money, no family to speak of. It's a strange case.'

'Aye, that's certainly true,' Bill commented amiably and took his leave. He tried to follow the direction that the policeman had indicated Sinclair's cottage lay in. After walking up and down a few back streets, the property turned out to be easy to locate. Again, the front door was conspicuously taped. Checking there was nobody around, Bill peered through the front window. The sitting room was messy and cramped. He tried the side gate and found it open. Bill slipped inside and walked down the side of the filthy white-washed building to the rear of the property.

The kitchen was housed in a small extension. Bill

tried the door but it was locked. He squinted through the window and discovered he could get a good view inside. Dirty plates and dishes were piled up in the sink. There was a cork board fixed to the wall next to the fridge. Bill edged closer and took a pencil and notebook out of his jacket pocket. There was a calendar with pictures of fishing boats on it pinned to the board, along with some dog-eared business cards. Bill jotted down every piece of information he could see, however trivial it seemed.

Suddenly, he heard the external door of the neighbouring cottage being opened. Bill crept back along the passageway, gently pulling the gate closed behind him, before casually setting off down the quaint little street, heading towards the harbour for his rendezvous with Rita at the museum.

Chapter Eight

The road where the Riddells lived had been long since gentrified. Most of the post-war housing boasted re-pointed brickwork. Every other residence possessed a loft conversion. DCs Andy Calder and Alice Mann approached the property which lay to the right of Fiona and Maisie's mid-terrace house. The occupants of the entire street had been questioned in the hours following the girl's disappearance but the DCI wanted them to speak again with the lad next door, whom Fiona had suggested was a friend of Maisie's.

A plump woman in her late forties answered. She led the two officers into the hallway and called upstairs to her son. Whilst they waited for Alex Ritchie to join them, his mother said in a lowered voice. 'You know that Alex isn't like other kids? I've never managed to get a proper diagnosis, mind you. But the school knows all about his condition. Just ask Mrs Boag.'

'You are entitled to be present for the entire interview, Mrs Ritchie,' Andy said.

She nodded, crossing her arms defensively. 'Don't worry, I certainly intend to be.'

Alex Ritchie was a big, solidly built lad. Andy estimated the boy was pushing six foot tall. He told them he was 16 years old and currently in Year 11 at Newton High School. Calder observed the young man closely. He could kind of tell what Mrs Ritchie meant. Alex was extremely fidgety. It took him a fraction of a second longer to answer a question than might normally be expected. However, both of these characteristics could also indicate a witness who was nervous; meaning he was either feeling guilty, lying, or both. Just because his mother told them Alex had special needs, it didn't mean Calder was prepared to rule out the latter possibility.

'Alex, could you please tell us again when you last saw Maisie Riddell.'

The boy's eyes darted back and forth. 'It was at school on Tuesday. I passed her in the playground. We said hello.'

'And you didn't see her at all on the Wednesday she went missing - not even during break time in the morning?' It was Alice Mann who posed this question.

Alex shook his head vigorously. 'No, I swear.'

'How would you describe your relationship with Maisie?'

'We weren't having a relationship!' The boy looked deeply alarmed.

'I just meant how good friends were you? How often did you speak with each other, did she confide in you, that sort of thing.'

Alex appeared to catch her drift. 'We listened to the same type of music. There's a band we both like called the Storm. We'd perform their stuff together sometimes.'

Alice turned towards Mrs Ritchie for clarification.

'Alex plays the acoustic guitar. It's the one thing he's really good at. Maisie sings. They used to perform cover versions of their favourite tracks. I wouldn't say they've done it quite so much in recent months but when they were younger they'd get together at least once a week,' the woman explained.

Alice glanced back at Alex. 'Why hadn't you and Maisie met up so much recently - had you fallen out?'

A look of pure misery passed across his face. 'She

just didn't want to do it anymore. Maisie always claimed she was busy with homework and stuff. Mum said she'd just grown out of it.'

'But you still talked to one another,' Andy put in.

'Oh yeah, we walked home from school together a lot. If I didn't have orchestra practice that was. We never planned to meet, but we were going the same way so it was bound to happen really, wasn't it?'

'Fiona doesn't get in until half past five most nights. Occasionally, Maisie would come in here with Alex and I'd fix them both a drink and a snack. She was always home well before her mum got back from work so I'm not sure she knew. I think Fiona would have felt awkward if she had, so I never mentioned it.' Mrs Ritchie seemed finally to have warmed up. She offered the detectives a coffee.

'No thank you,' Andy swiftly responded. 'Why do you think Fiona would have reacted badly to Maisie spending time at your house?'

'Well, it makes her look bad, doesn't it? I know the girl's fourteen but she still appreciated having some company when she got home from school.' Mrs Ritchie looked indignant.

'It sounds like you knew Maisie quite well. Did she mention anything to either of you about wanting to leave home?'

Mrs Riddell shook her head. 'No. She and her mum had their ups and downs. The walls between these houses are pretty thin. They had their arguments, but then so do we. Our children are teenagers. That's the way it goes. Fiona didn't have anyone at home to back her up or take the pressure off. It must be tough for her. But Maisie never said a word about leaving.'

Andy looked at Alex.

'No, Maisie didn't say anything to me either. I like Mrs Riddell. She's always really nice.'

'Okay, thank you both for your time. If Maisie does try to get in touch, please let us know straight away.' Andy handed Mrs Ritchie his card.

DCI Bevan was leading a briefing from Phil Boag's desk on the open-plan office floor of the Serious Crime Division.

'It can't be possible that Maisie Riddell simply vanished into thin air. Someone must have spotted her after she left the school gates. It is very unusual in the case of a runaway teenager to not find any footage of her getting onto a bus or a train. If she's still in the Glasgow area, then there must be a person out there who is sheltering her.'

'Or keeping her against her will,' Phil chipped in.

'Or she never made it out of the city because she's dead, Ma'am,' Alice Mann suggested.

Bevan nodded her head slowly. 'We can't rule out any of these scenarios. What about the boy next door, did he have anything new to add?'

Calder stepped forward. 'The boy knew Maisie a lot better than Fiona Riddell realised.'

Dani raised her eyebrows.

'I'm fairly sure it wasn't anything sexual. The pair played music together and hung out in his house after school. Mrs Ritchie was present most of the time. She claims she always checked on them regularly so nothing untoward went on. I don't reckon the boy would have been Maisie's type anyway. He's got learning difficulties and seems innocent in many ways.'

'But he's a big lad, Ma'am,' Alice interrupted. 'I'd say he's sexually mature but doesn't have the emotional maturity to go with it.'

Dani thought carefully about this. 'Could Alex Ritchie have physically overpowered Maisie?'

'Without a doubt,' Alice said resolutely. 'He's at

least six foot tall.'

'But the boy's gentle with it,' Andy added through gritted teeth, trying not to let his rising frustration show. 'He's a musical type, a member of the school orchestra and quite childlike. I can't imagine him becoming violent.'

'I could get Jane to give us a copy of the boy's file. That should provide a better picture of what the lad is capable of,' Phil suggested.

'Good idea, Phil. Could you arrange that for us?' Bevan asked.

Andy tossed his pen down onto the desk, where it landed with a loud clatter. 'I hope we aren't going to waste too much time on this line of inquiry Ma'am. I thought we'd moved on a bit as a force from fitting up the big lad next door with learning difficulties.'

Dani took a breath. She could sense the officers present waiting on tenterhooks to see what she would do next. 'Andy, could I have a word with you in my office please,' was all the DCI could say.

Chapter Nine

Dani gestured towards the sofa at the far end of her office and Andy took a seat.

He pre-empted his boss by saying, 'Sorry Ma'am. I shouldn't have been so flippant.'

'I don't mind hearing alternative views Andy, you know that. It's just a question of framing your objections in an appropriate way.' Bevan perched on the edge of her desk. 'But I understand it must be frustrating to be working alongside such a young and inexperienced officer as Alice yet being of the same rank.'

Andy looked up with a start, surprised that his superior officer was being so frank. 'Well, yes, actually it is. There's no way Alex Ritchie could have murdered Maisie Riddell and then got rid of her body. He may, at a pinch, have the physical strength to do it, but he doesn't have the personality traits. That's purely my instinct, of course.'

'Then I accept it's probably right. We'll take a look at his school records and that's it, we can put the inquiry to bed.'

'I'd just hate the press to get hold of the idea Alex is a suspect and then start vilifying the poor lad.'

Dani nodded. 'I'll tell the team to keep our interest in Alex Ritchie very quiet. Any news on the petrol receipts from Fiona's early morning jaunt on Wednesday?'

'Alice has got a print-out from the bank. Fiona paid for fifty quid's worth of fuel and a pint of milk. The transaction took place at 9.42am.'

'Okay. Make sure it gets added to the timeline.

That should be enough to clear the issue up.'

There was a knock at the door. Dani stood and let Phil Boag into the room.

'Sorry to interrupt, but there was something I wanted to mention out there and didn't get a chance.'

Dani raised her eyebrows quizzically.

'Georgina told me last night that Maisie thought her mother might have a boyfriend. It was purely a suspicion she had, because of Fiona's altered behaviour in recent weeks. Georgie didn't mention it to Andy as it was only a speculation.'

Dani dipped her head towards DC Calder. 'Let's go and have another word with Fiona Riddell.'

Charles Riddell was sitting at the kitchen table with a mug of coffee in front of him. His chin was sprinkled with several day's worth of salt and pepper stubble. Dani immediately imagined he must be staying in the house with his ex-wife. She wondered if he was sleeping in the spare room. Fiona offered the detectives a drink.

'Thank you, we'll both have a coffee,' Bevan responded warmly.

Charles gazed up at them like a puppy dog, with a look of desperate expectation on his drawn face.

'I'm sorry,' Dani quickly added. 'We've no news on Maisie's whereabouts. We just needed to ask you a couple more questions.'

The man slumped forward in a gesture of defeat.

Fiona was dressed in a figure-hugging woollen jersey and dark knee-length skirt. She looked smart and well groomed.

'We wondered if we might speak with you alone, Mrs Riddell,' Dani continued.

The woman hesitated, stirring milk into their

cups. 'Oh, of course. We could take our drinks into the lounge if you'd like?'

Charles didn't appear to notice them walk out.

Fiona sat stiffly in the armchair by the window, leaving her face in partial shadow. 'What's all this about?'

Andy took over. 'Have you been seeing anyone in recent months, Mrs Riddell?'

'Do I have to answer that question?' Fiona glanced at Dani.

'No, you aren't under any obligation to answer our questions. But absolutely any piece of information may be crucial to us finding your daughter, even if it seems trivial or unimportant to you.'

Fiona sighed. 'I went on one of those speed-dating evenings a couple of months back. I met a man there called Gavin. He seemed nice so we went out to dinner in town a couple of times. We didn't have much in common and we've not met up again. That's it.'

'Did Maisie meet this man?'

'No, absolutely not.'

'Can we have his full name and address please, so we can eliminate him from our inquiries?'

'I've only got his cell number, not his address.'

'That's fine. We'll be able to locate him from that.'

Fiona got up and retrieved a Filofax from a bureau next to the sofa. 'I don't see what this has got to do with Maisie. Why are you concentrating so many of your questions on me?'

For the first time, the woman looked really ruffled.

'It may seem that way,' Dani said. 'But I can assure you we are examining a number of different lines of inquiry.'

Fiona padded across the room and pushed the

door closed. 'I've been thinking,' she said carefully, resting her weight on the arm of a chair. 'Since Charles took that job at Barents Oil, he's been involved in some bad publicity over in Norway.'

'In what way?' Calder asked.

'Well, his company are at the forefront of the project to explore for oil in the Arctic Ocean, up near the Norwegian Archipelago. Greenpeace have been running a high profile campaign to have the exploration stopped. Charles has fronted a series of press conferences about it.'

Dani sat forward in her seat. 'Has your ex-husband ever received threats or been targeted by any groups over the issue?'

'I think he's mentioned getting letters and things. I didn't take much notice to be honest. I thought it was something for Kristin to worry about, not me. But what if one of these organisations has kidnapped Maisie? Maybe it's about time you started questioning Charles and his family, too.'

Charles Riddell tried his best to appear attentive. He listened impassively whilst Andy Calder laid out his ex-wife's concerns.

'I hadn't for a moment considered it might be an issue. These environmentalist groups are usually pacifists. Do you think they could have taken Maisie?'

'Have you ever received threatening messages?'

Charles nodded. 'Yes. We get them at work quite frequently. The IT department filters them out for us, so I never see them.'

'Do these messages threaten members of your family?'

'Not that I've ever seen. They are mostly highlighting the environmental damage caused by oil exploration – the destruction of the Arctic, that sort of thing. They aren't usually personal, otherwise I would have mentioned it sooner. If Maisie had been kidnapped, wouldn't we have received a demand of some kind by now? A pressure group would want to use the act for publicity, wouldn't they?'

Dani thought Charles was probably right and that this line of inquiry could prove to be a very costly diversion for her team. 'They may be planning the best possible moment to play their hand. Now that we've been provided with this information, we will have to sift through all of the malicious correspondence you've received at Barents Oil. We'll need the contact details of your IT department.'

Charles stood up heavily. 'I'll get it for you right now.'

Chapter Ten

An antiquated train-set filled the Hutchisons' spare room. Bill had spent the past couple of days perfecting the complex arrangement of tracks, points and tunnels, ready for his grandsons' visit at the weekend. He polished a Hornby Flying Scotsman with his sleeve and placed the engine down by one of the stations. Bill stood back to survey his work.

'It looks perfect.' Joy poked her head around the door. 'We'll never get the boys out of there.'

Her husband nodded with satisfaction.

When Joy had returned to stripping the beds in the guest room, Bill went downstairs and located his notebook by the telephone. He glanced again through the scribblings he had made at Terence Sinclair's property. From the research he had already done into the case online, Bill knew that Sinclair was 48 years old at the time of his death. He'd been married for ten years, but had divorced his wife five years ago. They'd had no children.

Bill was convinced that Richard Erskine was to blame for Sinclair's murder but he had yet to identify any kind of link between the two men. The way in which the boat-hand had been butchered and his body carefully placed fitted exactly with the circumstances of Mackie Shaw's death on Garansay just over a year ago, for which he and Bevan were certain Erskine was responsible. Bill knew that Erskine was still residing in his house in Inverness, living off his teacher's pension. Hutchison didn't have the time or the resources to observe how the man spent his days, but he would certainly like to.

One of the cards pinned to Sinclair's cork board was for a bar in Aberdeen. He'd jotted down the number and now he lifted the receiver to give the establishment a call.

'The Fisherman's Bar, how may I help you?' A woman's voiced answered.

'Oh, hello. Could you tell me what time you're open today?'

'We're doing lunches until 3 then we'll be closed 'till 6.30pm. After that we'll be serving until late. Did you want to book a table for food?'

'Are you expecting to be busy?'

'Not necessarily. But if you want to eat then you'd better come early. We've always got plenty of drinkers in after 8pm.'

'I got your number from a friend of mine, Terry Sinclair. He recommended your place.' Bill let the statement settle between them.

'Are you the press?' The woman asked tersely.

'No, not at all. My name is Bill and I was a neighbour of Terry's.'

The woman sighed heavily. 'I'm Liz. Terry used to come in here a lot. The regulars are pretty shaken up about his death. He was a harmless guy.'

'Did Terry have any particularly close drinking pals? I'm trying to get hold of some folk to attend his funeral. To be honest, he didn't have a great deal of friends here in Stonehaven.'

Liz thought for a moment. 'There's a few. If you give me your e-mail address then I'll send you their names. Better still, if you come in on a Friday night I'll introduce you to them. That was the evening Terry was always in here.'

'Thank you Liz. I will certainly do that.'

*

'Gavin Calhoun is forty six years old. He divorced three years ago and has two teenage sons. I spoke with him this afternoon.' Andy stepped into Dani's office and pulled the door shut.

'He confirms Fiona's story. He said they met twice for dinner and on the second occasion, Fiona told him that she would call him the following week to arrange another date, but she never did. That was the last contact they had.' Andy glanced at his notes. 'It was on January 23rd. Gavin said he'd heard about Maisie's disappearance on the news and considered sending Fiona a letter to say how sorry he was, but he hadn't done it yet. He claims he never came into contact with Fiona's daughter and she never met his sons. They didn't even go to each other's houses.'

'Did you believe him?'

'It's hard to say for sure with just one phone call but I didn't get the impression he was lying. He did add something interesting, though - as a sort of afterthought.'

'Oh, aye?' Dani leant forward.

'It could simply have been hurt male pride, but he said he was genuinely surprised that Fiona didn't get back in contact with him. Gavin felt they'd got on really well and there was a noticeable spark between them. He'd been deliberating calling her anyway, just to check everything was okay.'

'Well, it seems as if Fiona Riddell hadn't felt the same way.'

'No. How is the investigation into the environmental campaign against Barents Oil going?'

Dani let her eyes roll up towards the ceiling. 'Poor Phil is trawling through a mountain of material. I can't help thinking this is a total blind alley. If this case was a kidnapping we'd certainly have heard from the perpetrators by now.'

'Is Fiona Riddell trying to send us on a wild goose chase?'

Dani shrugged her shoulders. 'It could seriously reduce our chances of tracking down her daughter if she has.'

'You know, I'd really like to have a forensic team sweep through that house with a fine-toothed comb. Particularly to see if there's been any recent activity in the garden.' Andy looked at his boss expectantly.

'If we take that action, we'll have the national press swooping down on Fiona like feeding time at the zoo. We'd have to be bloody sure we thought she'd killed Maisie before we took that step. I don't feel certain enough of it just yet.'

Andy nodded. 'Okay. It's your call, Ma'am.'

Chapter Eleven

Dani could see her answering machine twinkling as soon as she stepped through the front door into the hallway. The Detective Chief Inspector decided to have something to eat before she listened to the messages.

About an hour later, in her dressing gown and slippers and with a mug of hot chocolate in her hand she sat on the stool by the phone and pressed the button. The first voice she heard was her father's. He was ringing from their home on the Isle of Colonsay, just making sure that she was well. The second message was from Bill, as she suspected it would be. A smile crept across her face as she listened to his exploits constructing an ancient train-set for his grandsons. As the message continued, her smile turned to a grimace and she reached for the receiver in frustration.

It was Joy who answered.

'Good evening, Joy. It's Dani Bevan here. How are you?'

'Oh, very well Detective Chief Inspector. I'm amazed to hear from you. I would have thought you'd be extremely busy right now.'

'I am,' she replied through gritted teeth. 'I wondered if I might have a quick word with Bill?'

Joy sounded surprised. 'Of course, I'll fetch him for you. He's just putting the finishing touches to a rather complicated diverging junction.'

'Inspector,' Bill said in a clipped tone. 'You got my message then?'

'Yes, I did.' She took a deep breath. 'Look, you

can't go interfering in a live murder inquiry. You could get into really serious trouble, Bill.'

'I've only been doing a little harmless digging. I know you are too wrapped up in this missing schoolgirl case to be able to devote any time to the investigation.'

'Even if I wasn't, I wouldn't be permitted to get involved in the Terence Sinclair murder inquiry. It's being handled by another division, with a different SIO. I have passed on the details of the Mackie Shaw case to DI Lyons. We can't do any more.'

'But I've come up with an interesting line of enquiry. It seems that Sinclair frequented a bar in Aberdeen. When I did some online checks into the place, I discovered that it had been raided on several occasions. It appeared that a number of the clientele had been involved in smuggling of various types. I really think it's worth looking into more deeply.'

'I'm sure that DI Lyons is already doing that, Bill. If you've discovered this piece of information, then they must have too.'

Bill let out a grunt that suggested he didn't share his friend's faith that this would necessarily be the case.

'Just be careful. Whoever murdered Terence Sinclair is clearly very dangerous. If there is smuggling involved then we're talking about organised crime. Terry might have been executed by a rival organisation. Isn't Louise bringing the boys down this weekend?'

'Yes,' Bill was forced to admit.

'Then forget all about it for the time being, okay?'

'Alright, DCI Bevan. I shall.'

'Good, and for heaven's sake just call me Dani, will you?'

*

Bevan settled into the chair opposite her Detective Sergeant, recalling the time when they shared a desk together and feeling the pang of nostalgia.

Phil fished a pile of photocopies out of his briefcase and handed them to her. 'Jane said she knows Alex Ritchie and his parents well. He's attended the school since Year 7. His mum has been trying hard to get him a statement of special needs since that time.'

'What exactly is his issue?'

Phil relaxed back into his seat. 'He's not an easy boy to slot into a comfortable category, which is why Debbie Ritchie has never been given her statement from the local authority. Jane suggests that Alex is emotionally immature and his IEP states that his processing skills are slow. He has a reading age of 11.'

'Does Alex have any history of violence? What is Jane's opinion of the lad – does she think he *could* be violent?'

Phil shook his head. 'Alex is a gentle boy. Jane used the word 'withdrawn' to describe him at school. He's never been violent towards other children, although he has suffered himself from a certain amount of bullying by the other kids. Jane said that even if he'd done something to Maisie, Alex wouldn't be capable of keeping it quiet for very long.'

'Okay, this confirms Andy's assessment of the lad. I had thought that perhaps Maisie had confided in Alex about what she had planned, or even how she was making this extra cash that she had. But with Jane's testimony, I think it's unlikely. Maisie would have known that Alex couldn't keep a secret, even if he'd wanted to.'

'She definitely didn't tell Georgina what she'd been up to. I'd know by now if she had.'

'What about the Norwegian line of enquiry?'

Phil sighed. 'DC Clifton and I are still going through all the letters and e-mails. Very few are directed towards specific individuals at Barents Oil. Most are propaganda pieces about the dangers to wildlife and the eco-system if drilling were to take place in the Arctic Ocean. There *were* a slew of e-mails directed at Charles Riddell, just after he fronted a press conference last year. Most were from high profile environmental groups but a couple were anonymous.'

'Were they threatening in any way?'

Phil pulled a face. 'Not directly, although they certainly weren't complimentary.'

'Could you print off copies of all the anonymous messages? I'd like to see the wording of those.'

'Sure. I can't see any of the established environmentalist groups being involved in a kidnapping. These days they have a great deal of funding and tend to fight their battles through the courts, invoking International Law. The abduction of a teenager doesn't quite fit with that approach.'

'No, but Charles may have riled up some radical fringe group. There are criminal organisations out there that simply look for a righteous cause to give their actions credibility.' Dani made to stand up.

'I'll get a print-out ready for you by lunchtime.'

Bevan took a couple of paces towards her office. Phil halted her progress by suddenly saying, 'Ma'am, don't you get the sense that all we're doing is closing down possibilities? It feels as if we're actually getting even further away from finding Maisie.'

Dani paused for a second and then, as if her sergeant hadn't spoken, she got on with the work of the day.

Chapter Twelve

There wasn't a plausible reason that Bill could think of for why he might be taking a trip to Aberdeen on a Friday evening. He was forced to tell Joy the truth instead. She was not as condemnatory as Bill had expected. In fact, his wife was less alarmed by her husband's inquiries into the death of Terence Sinclair and more concerned about his plan to visit a pub frequented by criminal types.

'The landlady sounded perfectly nice on the phone. I've already introduced a good cover story,' Bill insisted, as he gathered together his coat and bag.

Joy furrowed her brow. 'Louise will be here early in the morning. What will I tell her if something happens to you?'

Bill paused from his preparations and put his arms around her. 'I'm going to be fine. I shall simply ask a few innocent questions, dear. I'm fairly inconspicuous. I'm quite obviously not a police officer or private investigator.'

Joy wasn't sure that was actually a good thing, but she forced a smile and gave Bill a peck on the cheek before he slipped out of the door.

The Fisherman's Bar was in a run-down building not far from the harbour. Bill couldn't imagine for a second that anyone would wish to come to the place for their evening meal. It struck him immediately as a hard-core drinking establishment, for those individuals working at the docks, perhaps. The windows contained panes of almost opaque glass, like the bases of milk bottles. Bill couldn't make out a single thing on the other side of them. It made him distinctly nervous, but he took a deep breath and pushed through the heavy door.

The light inside was dim and the décor reminded Bill of a working men's club he'd been taken into once by a friend in Stirling. He immediately approached the wood cladded bar. A forty-something woman was serving drinks to a group of men. She was thin and her face heavily lined, a strappy top dotted with sparkly sequins hung off her bony frame. When she'd finished with the customers, the woman turned towards Bill.

'Liz?' He enquired. 'We spoke on the telephone a couple of days ago. I'm Bill Hutchison. I was a friend of Terry's.'

The woman cracked a smile. 'Oh aye, I remember. Can I get you something?'

'A pint of 70 shilling please.' He decided it would be best to drink what everyone else was, although he could really have done with a stiff brandy.

'Sure.' Liz reached for a clean glass and placed it under a pump with no discernible markings. 'It's a bit early yet, but when Terry's cronies come in, I'll give you the nod. Okay?'

Bill took his pint over to a small table where he could observe the rest of the pub. There was a television set high up in one corner, showing an obscure sporting event. A pool table was accommodated in a dark alcove at the opposite side of the room. This was where the scant clientele had congregated, leaning in close and speaking in low voices. None of them were yet playing a game.

Half an hour later, Bill took his empty glass back to Liz for a re-fill. As he stood at the counter, trying to avoid resting his sleeve in a puddle of beer, another group of men arrived. Liz greeted them warmly and automatically supplied her new customers with drinks, indicating that these gentlemen were regulars. She even took their brimming glasses over to them on a circular tin tray, of the type Bill hadn't seen in several decades. Not since his mother had been the stewardess of a Golf Club in Helensburgh. When Liz was re-installed behind the pumps, she nodded to the group she'd just served.

'Those folk knew Terry. The tall one is called Stewart. If you mention there'll be a free spread and some liquid *hospitality* on offer, you'd definitely get that lot to the poor guy's funeral.'

Bill took a swig of his ale, suddenly thinking this may not have been such a good idea. Before giving himself chance to back out, he picked up his glass and strode across to their table.

The three men eyed him suspiciously.

'Good evening. My name is Bill. I was a neighbour of Terry Sinclair. Liz told me that you were friends of his too?'

A silence surrounded them that was so thick, Bill almost felt as if he could slice through it with a knife.

'Are you from the paper's pal?' One of the men finally demanded.

'Oh no. I retired a few years ago now. I was the bookkeeper for a furniture factory in Stirling.'

'He wasn't asking for your life story,' the man who Liz referred to as Stewart added with a snort, eliciting raucous laughter from the other men. 'Come on, take a seat.'

Bill lowered himself carefully onto a stool, placing his drink on the tiny table.

'I'm Stewart, this is Dougie and Paul. We used to drink with Terry on a Friday night. If you don't mind me saying, Bill. You don't look like the type of fella Terry usually hung out with.'

'Oh, my wife and I were simply his neighbours, but we got to know each other quite well.'

'Are you the couple with the grandchildren?'

Bill nodded, without elaborating.

'Oh aye, Terry said you were all right.'

'Yes, well, we're organising a gathering down in Stonehaven for Terry. After the police finally release his body and allow the funeral to go ahead. I've been trying to track down some of his pals to come along for the send-off. Terry didn't appear to have many close family members.'

The three men nodded solemnly. 'He went through a nasty divorce. Terry's been pretty much on his own ever since.'

'So there isn't any chance his ex-wife would come to the funeral?'

Stewart snorted again. 'Michelle's long off the scene. Terry would barely have her name mentioned after she left.'

'Did Terry ever do any work up here in Aberdeen? There may be some colleagues around the city who would want to pay their respects.'

Stewart narrowed his eyes suspiciously. 'Are you sure you're no' the polis?'

Bill chuckled, as confidently as he could manage, 'of course not.'

Stewart slapped him hard on the back, causing Bill to spill a small amount of his beer. 'I'm only joking, pal. You certainly don't look like the polis.'

'Had Terry ever been a fisherman himself?' Bill wondered out loud.

'I think his father was,' Dougie put in. 'He grew up in Stonehaven. When I met Terry he was living here in Aberdeen. He did odd jobs for various folk back then, cash in hand mostly. It was always to do with the boats, though.'

'He doesn't strike me as a person anybody would want to kill,' Bill muttered quietly.

Stewart leaned in close, his beery breath tickling the older man's cheek. 'Terry had his finger in a lot of pies. I wasn't really that surprised to find out he'd been done over. Not surprised at all.'

Bill had taken a number from Stewart and promised to call him about Sinclair's wake. He returned to the bar. Suddenly hungry, he asked Liz if they were still serving food.

'I could do you sausage and chips?' She suggested.

'That would be perfect, thanks,' Bill replied, trying to peer behind her into the kitchen area. All the doors leading back there were firmly closed.

The voices of the men around him were growing increasingly louder as the evening wore on and the beers were replaced by stubby tumblers of whisky. Bill's food arrived. A young woman in an apron passed it to Liz through a serving hatch. The girl's striking appearance caught his attention. She was blond-haired and blue-eyed, looking to Bill to be extremely youthful.

He finished up his plate of food, adding conversationally, 'that was great, just what I needed. My compliments to the chef.'

Liz nodded. 'I'll tell Keith, he'll be pleased. Most of the folk in here barely notice what they're shovelling down their necks.'

'I thought the girl may have been the one doing the cooking?'

Liz stopped wiping down the bar and looked at him closely. 'Anita just helps us out. She washes the dishes and collects the empties.'

'I see.' Bill polished off his pint and gathered his

things together.

'Are you off?' Liz asked flatly.

'Aye, my daughter is coming early to visit in the morning. I can't stay any longer.'

'Well, maybe next time you'll not need to rush away so quickly,' she said cryptically. Then Liz fished a crisp business card from a pile on the back of the bar, just like the one pinned to Terry Sinclair's notice board. 'If you've enjoyed your evening and want to do it again, give me a call. Any friend of Terry's is always welcome here.'

Chapter Thirteen

Andy Calder returned to his modern first floor flat in the west-end of Glasgow at just before seven. Carol had already put Amy down to sleep in her cot and Andy knew to enter through the front door as quietly as possible.

He removed his coat and shoes and padded into the small, functional kitchen. Carol was stirring a pot on the stove. Andy put his arms around her from behind and rested his face against hers.

'Have you had a good day?'

'Aye. Amy and I went to the drop-in clinic this morning.'

Andy's posture stiffened. 'Is everything okay?'

'It was just to get her weighed and for a chat with the health visitors. She's perfectly fine.'

Andy went into the main bedroom and changed out of his suit. Making his way towards the small lounge he ducked his head into his daughter's nursery, gazing for a moment at her peaceful form.

He was still smiling as he turned on the television set and positioned himself comfortably on the sofa in front of it. Andy just caught the end of the local news and discovered Jane Boag staring out of the screen at him. The detective sensed Carol come into the room.

'She's a real ball-breaker that one,' he muttered quietly.

'I was just thinking how glamorous she looked,' Carol replied, taking in the woman's tall, slim physique, displayed to full advantage in an expensively tailored suit and with sleek black hair pinned up expertly to frame her attractive face. Carol subconsciously placed a hand to her own ample, post-baby curves.

'Jane is certainly not *my* type,' Andy put in forcefully. 'She's all spiky edges, in more ways than one.'

The Headmistress was being interviewed about yet another proposed slew of changes to the examination system. Jane was commenting on how the reforms did nothing to address the fact that current education policies were failing to engage modern children.

'She's got a good point,' Carol said. 'These politicians are so out of touch.'

Andy creased his face into a frown. 'A young girl is still missing from Jane's school - out there somewhere in the dark and cold. All *she* can talk about are bloody government initiatives.'

'That's her job. The world can't stop turning because Maisie Riddell's run away from home.'

Andy pulled his wife onto the sofa next to him and gave her a tight squeeze, thinking about their own little girl, lying in her soft pink pyjamas, all safe and warm in her room down the corridor. 'I don't know,' he said with a sigh. 'Perhaps it really should.'

*

As DCI Bevan exited the lift and strode across the open-plan floor of the Serious Crime Division, she noted that DS Boag was the first at his desk again. Dani called out, 'good morning!' as she passed him and proceeded into her own office. The phone started ringing as soon as the detective sat down.

It was the reception desk, informing Bevan that Charles Riddell was waiting in the lobby to see her.

Apparently, he was in something of a state. Dani immediately jumped up, pulling on her jacket once again and summoning Phil to accompany her downstairs.

Mr Riddell was sitting on the edge of a soft chair by the entrance doors with his head resting in his hands. Dani slowly approached the man, clearing her throat as she got closer. Charlie looked up, his face pinched with anguish.

'Has something happened, Mr Riddell?' She asked gently.

He nodded.

Phil led them towards one of the more pleasant of the ground floor interview rooms. There was a three piece suite in this one and a small window. They all took a seat.

'I need to ask your permission to return to Norway, Detective Chief Inspector. I'm booked on the next flight.' Charlie gazed at her pleadingly.

'Of course,' she replied, 'you aren't a suspect.'

'Thank you,' the man let out a huge sigh of relief. 'Kristin called me this morning. She is very upset. There was an incident at the house yesterday.'

'What kind of incident?' Phil enquired gravely, getting out his notebook.

'It was late afternoon and the temperature was extremely mild. My wife had left Gabriel in the buggy to sleep. He was on the step by the front door. She had kept the door open but was pottering around inside the kitchen for a few moments.' Charles glanced up and caught Dani's eye. 'We do not have any near neighbours. Our house is on the edge of the forest.'

'Carry on.'

'When she came out to check on Gabriel, she found the buggy was gone. At first, Kristin thought she may not have secured the brake properly and it had rolled down the driveway a little, so that it was out of sight. But when she rushed outside, the baby was nowhere to be seen. Kristin was frantic, as you can imagine. She ran up and down the track which leads to the main road, searching for him. After ten minutes, she called the police. They sent a car very quickly and several officers scoured the surrounding area. They found Gabriel some forty five minutes later. His buggy was semi-hidden in a little dip in the woods, about half a mile from the house. My little boy was still asleep. He appeared totally unharmed.'

Dani edged forwards. 'Do the Norwegian authorities have any idea who was responsible?'

Charles shook his head, looking confused. 'Not yet, they are investigating the woods thoroughly. Kristin says officers are still at the house. Do you think this could have something to do with Maisie's disappearance? Is there someone out there targeting me?' The man seemed extremely agitated.

'We'd need to look into this more closely to be able to say,' Dani explained. 'But it is certainly possible.'

68

Chapter Fourteen

'Was Carol okay about you coming away at such short notice?' Bevan asked her colleague, as they hauled their baggage through Stavanger Airport.

'Her mother is going to stay for a couple of days. Carol's fine, she knows it's all part of the job.'

Their hotel was a short taxi drive away. Once they'd had a chance to freshen up, Dani and Andy made their way to the police headquarters, where the British detectives would be liaising with the National Criminal Investigation Service.

The headquarters were housed in an impressive glass-fronted building, positioned just on the outskirts of the city. Stavanger was a low-lying settlement, with a largely coastal landscape. The urban area was surrounded by the sea, five lakes and three fjords, with the centre of the town retaining much of its period charm. Dani already knew that the offices of Barents Oil were based in a nearby business park. But she wanted to speak with the investigating officer in charge of the Riddell case before she paid a visit there.

Dani and Andy were greeted by a tall man in his early forties who introduced himself as Detective Dieter Karlsen. Bevan was relieved to note that he spoke impeccable English. They were led up an escalator to a mezzanine level where several glass topped desks were populated by busy looking staff. Detective Karlsen introduced them to a younger woman, apparently his partner. Her name was Magda Hustad.

'Have you already been briefed on our missing

person case in Glasgow?' Dani enquired.

'Yes,' said Karlsen. 'Your colleague Phil Boag has sent us an account of Maisie Riddell's disappearance. I studied the details this morning.'

'Good. Could you give us a run-down of the investigation into the attempted abduction of Gabriel?'

Karlsen nodded towards Magda who led them over to a large desk area. She picked up a handful of photographs, obviously taken of the Riddell's property and the surrounding terrain. 'This is the spot where our men found the little boy and his pram. There was no evidence that he had been disturbed in any way. Kristin Riddell claimed his clothing and blankets were exactly as she had left them.'

'So what was the purpose of hiding the boy? Was the intention to frighten the Riddells?' Andy asked.

Magda nodded. 'At this stage we think that must have been the case. He was only a half mile from the house. The boy was never in any great danger.'

'Perhaps the abductor was interrupted and simply decided to abandon the plan, dumping Gabriel and fleeing the scene. Maybe whoever it was had not expected the mother to come out of the house again so quickly. The perpetrator might have seen her from the woods and decided to abort the kidnapping.'

'That is also a possibility,' Karlsen added, 'especially if the same people are responsible for the kidnapping of Maisie Riddell. It shows that they are perfectly capable of abducting a child.'

'But taking an eighteen month old toddler is an entirely different proposition from holding a teenager,' Andy commented.

'And no effort has been made by any group to take the credit for Maisie's disappearance, whereas this act seems to be directed quite specifically at Charles Riddell,' Dani supplied.

'Perhaps it is part of an escalating series of events,' Karlsen explained. 'Maisie's fate was just the start. As the acts become more frequent then the aims of the perpetrators will be made apparent.'

Dani nodded, this theory was certainly plausible, especially if it was the work of an extremist organisation setting out to make a big impact. 'Do you have any idea which pressure groups may have decided to target Charles Riddell?' Bevan glanced at Detective Karlsen.

'As your Sergeant has been doing, we too have looked into the threats received by all of the executives working at Barents Oil. We were quite amazed by the sheer number there has been in the past few years. Some of the individuals responsible are known to us, we have detailed files on a few.'

Magda Hustad retrieved more documents from the glass topped desk. A mug shot was paper-clipped to the corner of a detailed form sitting at the top of the pile. Dani examined the face closely. This individual was not more than a teenager, she thought.

'This is Andreas Nilsen. He started out as a student campaigner, but as far as we can tell, he has never taken a proper job since graduation,' Magda explained. 'Nilsen has been arrested several times for petty offences, such as the damaging of oil executives' cars.'

'Has he ever been in direct contact with Riddell?' Dani asked.

Karlsen nodded. 'That's why we picked him out of the bunch. Nilsen's environmental group were sending propaganda e-mails to Charles Riddell even when he was still working in Scotland.'

Bevan tipped her head towards Calder and

scooped up her bag. 'Does this individual live close by?'

'About a twenty minute drive away,' the Norwegian detective confirmed.

Detective Hustad remained at headquarters, helping the team to continue sifting through the many protest e-mails and letters received over the past few years by the Barents Oil Corporation. Dani sat beside Dieter Karlsen in the front of his estate car. Andy Calder was leaning forward from his position on the backseat, so he could hear what the local cop was telling them.

'Riddell's wife was previously known as Kristin Berg. She was also an employee at Barents Oil. She was one of Charles' secretaries, although she left the corporation not long after marrying her boss. The baby was born a year or so later.'

'It makes sense that the guy met his new partner on the job. Apparently, Charles Riddell puts a lot of hours in,' Andy added. 'That's why his first wife left him.'

Karlsen nodded sagely. 'It is a situation that policemen know a great deal about.'

Dani looked at her companion closely. At least two day's worth of stubble covered the lower half of his face, but the man's hair was neatly trimmed and his shirt carefully ironed. He wore a thick gold band on the third finger of his right hand, as was customary for married men in Norway.

'What did you make of Kristin Riddell when you spoke to her? Did she strike you as the ditsy type? Might she have forgotten leaving the pram in the woods? Perhaps she'd taken the baby for a walk and lost her bearings. The story of the buggy being left outside on the driveway may have been a fabrication, to excuse her own negligence,' Dani suggested, thinking out loud.

Karlsen shot her a sideways glance, with watery, grey-green eyes. 'The woman was frantic about the child. I believe she genuinely thought he had been abducted.'

Dani nodded. She didn't need any further convincing. Bevan suspected that Dieter Karlsen's instincts were razor sharp.

Within a few moments, they pulled up onto a steep drive which sat at the foot of a single-level property, perched in an impressive position on the mountainside, overlooking a perfectly still lake.

'Does Nilsen live *here*?' Andy asked incredulously, surveying the collection of BMWs parked in front of the garage.

'He still lives with his parents.' When Dani raised an eyebrow at this, Nilsen said, 'I never suggested the guy was a master criminal. None of these young eco-warrior types really are.'

They climbed a set of stone steps which led to the front door. Andy turned for a moment and absorbed the stunning view before spinning back and folding his arms across his chest.

A slim, blond woman answered the door. She was dressed in a roll neck sweater and dark jeans but managed to make this simple ensemble appear incredibly chic.

Karlsen addressed the woman in Norwegian. Dani heard the detective mention her son's name. The woman stood back and muttered a protest. Somehow Dani sensed that the family had guests. They were led into a bright and open plan kitchen. Just as Bevan had predicted, there were plates of food and open bottles of wine covering the central island. Karlsen began speaking in English.

'Mrs Nilsen, there was an incident yesterday that we need to ask Andreas some questions about.'

The woman sighed heavily. 'Stay in here would you? I'll send him in. But please could you keep it short? We are having a lunch party for my husband's birthday.'

'Of course.'

Andreas Nilsen strode in a few moments later, carrying a glass of champagne and grinning from ear to ear. He greeted the detective in his native language, in a relaxed manner that suggested to Dani the young man knew him well.

'These are two of my colleagues from Glasgow, they are assisting my investigation,' Karlsen said.

Andreas raised his flute in a gesture of welcome, not appearing in the least bit perturbed. 'Good. I will get a chance to practise my English.'

Karlsen was beginning to get annoyed. 'When did you last send hate mail to Charles Riddell, Andreas?'

The young man tipped his face towards the ceiling, as if trying to recall the details of a pleasant holiday excursion or day trip. 'Not for at least six months. I've been busy with other ventures.'

'A couple of days ago, the Riddells' baby boy was taken from outside the family's home.' Karlsen allowed this piece of information to sink in. Dani felt sure she saw a flicker of emotion pass across the lad's features.

'Oh yes,' Andreas replied, his face fixed in a rictus grin. 'What's that got to do with me?'

Dani stepped forward. 'Why did you target Charles Riddell when he was working in Aberdeen? What did he do to catch your attention?'

The young man allowed his piercing blue eyes to slide down the contours of her slim, athletic frame. If the gesture was intended to intimidate her, it hadn't worked. 'Our friend Charlie wrote a scientific paper back in 2007, suggesting that the future of international oil exploration should be focused on the Arctic Ocean. He claimed that Norwegian oil companies should be at the forefront of this project. Since that time, the man has been at the top of my Christmas card list.'

'You must have been particularly annoyed when Riddell came to work here, then?' Andy put in casually.

'Not at all,' Andreas laughed and took a long sip of champagne. 'It merely saved money on the postage.'

Karlsen leaned forward and Dani saw that his face was flushed with anger. 'Do you know what the penalty is for child abduction - particularly of a baby? Your pretty boy looks wouldn't serve you very well in prison.'

Andreas blinked several times, but his expression remained blank. 'I had absolutely nothing to do with that. It's not my style.' He gestured around him. 'I live with my parents, where on earth could I hide a baby?'

'You've got associates,' Karlsen replied levelly.

'My group are made up of student-types, mostly girls. They wouldn't want any part in the kidnapping of a young child.'

'Do you know Maisie Riddell?' Dani suddenly asked, examining those dazzling blue eyes closely.

Andreas shook his thick head of sandy hair. 'No. Is she a relative of Charles? I'm aware the baby is a boy, but that's all I know.'

'We've got a warrant to seize your computer and phone,' Karlsen added.

'Fine, but I need them returned to me by tomorrow afternoon. I'll get my lawyer onto it.'

'You do that,' Karlsen snapped.

The lad padded out of the kitchen and returned a few moments later with the devices. He seemed to have regained some of his composure. As he handed them over to the detective he said conversationally, 'and how is *Mrs* Karlsen these days?'

The officer flashed Andreas a look of pure hatred, thanked him through gritted teeth for his assistance and led his two colleagues back out to the car.

Bevan was sure that Detective Karlsen was driving more aggressively on the return route to Stavanger.

'Did you think he was lying?' Andy asked generally.

Bevan directed her response to the Norwegian officer. 'You know him best, Dieter, but I thought the news about Gabriel Riddell was completely unexpected.'

Karlsen nodded. 'I agree. Much as I dislike Nilsen and his cronies, I don't think they've got the gumption to pull off this kind of thing, particularly not the abduction of Maisie from a totally different country. It's way out of Andreas' league.'

'And there aren't any other organisations you think could be responsible?'

'There are still a few individuals I'd like to question, but none of them has the kind of record I'd associate with a child kidnapping.'

Bevan gazed out of the window, watching the snow-capped mountains zig-zagging across the horizon. The sun was liquefying into a narrow strip of orange behind their darkening peaks. 'Do you know Andreas personally? Why did he ask about your wife?'

Karlsen was silent for a moment before responding. 'Sofie works for another oil company in Stavanger. It is one of Barents' competitors. She's a scientist. Sofie is also on Andreas Nilsen's Christmas card list.'

Bevan nodded her head with understanding but said nothing. Calder shuffled back into his seat and stared out of the window. The car then proceeded in the direction of the outskirts of the town, without the occupants uttering another word.

Chapter Fifteen

The landscape always appeared quite different after a heavy frost, Bill thought to himself, as he pulled back the curtains in their bedroom. Joy was already downstairs making tea. Bill glanced up and down the quiet street, his eyes lingering for a moment when he spotted something out of place.

One of the cars parked on the kerbside was not covered in a layer of silvery-white dust like the others. The windscreen of the Ford Focus sitting opposite their house was clear and a thin sliver of exhaust could be seen snaking from the rear. Bill peered more closely. He made out the bulky figure of a person seated behind the wheel, bundled up in padded clothing and totally impassive. Bill took a note of the number plate before pulling on his dressing gown and going downstairs to join his wife.

Joy immediately poured him a cup of tea from the pot. 'What's the matter? You look terribly pale.'

'There's a car outside in the road. Someone's watching the house.'

Joy automatically put a hand up to the frilly neckline of her full-length nightgown. 'How do you know?'

'He's sitting out there with the engine running. There are no tyre marks in the frost. I think he's been there all night.' Bill furrowed his brow in a deep frown.

'Who on earth could it be?'

Bill shook his head solemnly and then jumped out of his seat, striding into the hallway and dragging on his thick overcoat and boots. 'I don't know, but I'm going to find out.'

But by the time Bill had marched out of the front door and reached the pavement, the car was nowhere in sight. Only a rectangle of dark tarmac amidst the sea of white indicated where the vehicle had once been.

*

Dani was beginning to understand why everyone in Scandinavia wore a woollen sweater underneath their jackets for work. In her thin blouse and cardigan, she was bloody freezing. Bevan went back to her hastily packed case and rummaged through the contents. She discovered a shapeless, ribbed burgundy roll necked jumper that she rarely wore, largely because it was so unflattering, unbuttoned her shirt and pulled on the thicker garment instead.

When Bevan entered the hotel's dining room for breakfast, she noted that Andy had also dressed more warmly today. He was wearing a cable-knitted jumper with little snowflake motifs, which looked very much like an unwelcome Christmas present from a time before he'd lost all the weight.

'Don't say a word, Ma'am. I didn't think I would actually need to wear it.'

Dani smiled but said nothing, pouring herself a coffee instead and selecting a large pastry from the basket in the centre of the table.

'So, what's the plan this morning?' Andy glanced at his boss over a spoonful of cereal.

'Karlsen and Hustad are going to question some more leaders of local environmentalist groups. We are going to pay a visit to Barents Oil.'

'Do you think Dieter is the right person to be leading the investigation - isn't he too close to the oil business?'

'I suspect his wife's job gives him a good perspective on the whole thing. I get the sense he's a decent cop.'

'But what's happening to Charlie Riddell's family must be making him nervous. I wonder if the Karlsens have got any kids themselves.'

Bevan shrugged her shoulders and drained her coffee cup. 'Come on, let's get going. The headquarters are only a short walk from here.'

The security at Barents Oil was tight. Despite showing their IDs, the British detectives had to empty out the contents of their bags and submit to being patted down by a burly guard in uniform. They were then escorted to the senior executive's office by a secretary who said nothing until she had reached the door, where she gave a sharp knock and introduced them to her boss as police officers.

Emrik Hansen was in his mid-fifties, but he was trim and sported a fashionable hair-cut and designer glasses. He greeted them warmly. 'Please take a seat. I'm keen to help Charles to clear up this unpleasant matter. I've told him to work from home for the time being, so that he can be with Kristin and Gabriel.'

'Is it usual for your executives to receive threats and hate mail?' Andy Calder asked.

Hansen leant forward, adopting an earnest expression. 'Unfortunately, yes. It is the nature of the job. My IT department do their very best to filter the worst of it out. I rarely see any unpleasant material addressed to myself, although I am in no doubt that it is sent on a regular basis.'

'Had there ever been attacks on your employees before this?'

The CEO pursed his lips. 'I wouldn't be too quick to assume that Charles' problems relate to his work here at Barents. In answer to your question, about two years ago, the windscreens of the management team's cars were smashed in, whilst they were outside in the car park. We had CCTV footage of the incident, but the perpetrators wore hoods pulled low over their faces. Within a few days, a local environmentalist group claimed responsibility. I believe the police prosecuted a couple of young men for criminal damage.'

'Nothing else?' Andy pressed, having already viewed the details of the incident back at the Criminal Investigation Bureau.

Hansen reclined in his chair, evidently thinking this through. 'Not here at Barents. I do recall something involving a scientist at one of the other oil corporations in Stavanger a little while ago. We aren't the only show in town, detectives.' The man gave a thin smile. 'Can I get Maya to bring us some refreshments?'

'That won't be necessary,' Bevan said quickly. 'We'd like to take a look at Mr Riddell's office now please.'

'You can tell Charlie Riddell's a Scot. He hasn't got the minimalist thing going that all the other offices seem to have,' Andy commented, as he sifted through the items on the desk wearing his latex gloves.

'Yes, there's quite a lot of clutter. He must drive his secretary mad.' Dani examined the framed photographs that Riddell kept on his workstation. One was a studio shot of a very pretty blonde woman cradling a newborn baby. The other was of Charlie with an arm placed firmly around Maisie's shoulders. There was a fantastic backdrop of fjords and mountains behind them and the girl was beaming contentedly for the camera. Dani pointed at the picture saying, 'that's the happiest I've ever seen her.'

'I wonder if it was taken before or after her dad

had another child,' Andy said quietly. 'Maisie looks quite young there.'

Bevan noted the half bottle of Scotch stored at the back of one of the fitted cupboards and took a few pictures on her phone of the more recent documents that Riddell had been working on. After this, she decided it was time for them to make tracks back to the Bureau. A different, but equally taciturn secretary saw the detectives out of the building. There was no sign of Emrik Hansen as they were guided through the huge, glass fronted lobby.

Chapter Sixteen

Karlsen and Hustad had arrived back just before their British colleagues. Magda looked at Dani and crinkled up her face. 'None of the pressure groups known to us is admitting to targeting the Riddells. I can't see the point of any of these crimes if the organisations responsible aren't getting any publicity out of it.'

'Unless they're trying to pressurize Charles into doing something for them,' Andy responded. 'What is he currently working on?'

Dani said, 'I looked through Charles' inbox at Barents Oil. I must admit I didn't understand much of it, but his recent correspondence seemed to relate to the choice of contractors for their latest exploration site. We could always question Riddell on it further.'

Karlsen nodded. 'That's an excellent idea. These contracts are fought over in a very competitive way. There is a great deal of money available for the drilling companies who are awarded a deal. Good thinking, Detective Calder.' The Norwegian officer placed his hand on Andy's shoulder.

Bevan perched on the edge of a desk, feeling the discomfort of its sharp angles. 'The CEO at Barents mentioned an incident involving a scientist at one of the other oil companies in Stavanger. He intimated it may have been linked to the environmentalists.'

Magda shot her superior a sideways glance. 'He must have been referring to Aron Holm.' She didn't elaborate on the statement, so Bevan looked towards Dieter to tell her more.

'Holm is the Chief Scientific Officer at Skaldic Oil Conglomerates. Eighteen months ago, he was attacked when he returned to his car which was parked outside a restaurant in the town. It occurred down an alleyway where one of the street lights was out of order. Holm was very badly beaten. The man was in hospital for a couple of weeks. He has fully recovered now.'

Dani slowly rose to a standing position, wondering why they were only hearing about this now. 'Did you make an arrest?'

Dieter shook his head. 'We questioned many people involved in the environmental movement but just like now, we found no solid connection to the assault. There was no CCTV camera where it happened and not a single witness came forward. Holm said his attacker was wearing a balaclava which covered his face.' The Norwegian policeman cleared his throat. 'My wife works in Holm's department. They were all very shaken up by the incident, so I can assure you that we took it extremely seriously.'

'I'd like to speak with Mr Holm, if that's possible,' Dani stated.

'If you believe it is necessary then I can set up a meeting.'

'I do think it's necessary, yes.' Bevan tried very hard to keep the frustration out of her voice.

*

Skaldic Oil Conglomerates operated out of a more traditional building than its rival, closer to the older part of Stavanger. Holm's office was in a small room on one of the top floors. Bevan caught a glimpse of an impressive view from out of the louvred window. Dani noted that this was every bit the domain of a scientist. Textbooks lined the wooden shelves and pieces of laboratory equipment filled every available space on the floor.

The Scientific Officer himself was aged in his late-fifties. His white hair was thick and obviously in need of a cut but the man's face wore a broad smile. 'So, you are here from Glasgow,' he stated. 'I lived in Maryhill for a few years in the early 90s. I was a visiting lecturer at the university. I have happy memories of the place.' Holm gestured for them to take a seat.

'I'm sorry to be bringing up such an unpleasant incident again, Mr Holm, but as Detective Karlsen may have told you, we think that an oil executive in Stavanger is being targeted by an extremist group. There might be a connection to the attack on you.'

The scientist sat down heavily in his chair. 'I will be honest with you, it is an episode of my life that I would dearly love to forget. There was never any evidence that environmentalists were responsible for the assault on me.'

Andy leant forward, placing his elbows on his knees. 'Did you receive any threatening communications in the weeks and months leading up to the day you were attacked?'

Holm ran a hand through his snowy locks. 'I did go through all of this with the detectives at the time. My department was working on a technique for creating a synthetic substitute for crude oil. It was a highly secretive project at the time, although we now have a patent for the product. Within a decade, it should be in limited commercial use. My approach is based on the Fischer-Tropsch process, first pioneered in Germany between the wars, but it incorporates a simplification of our current methods of oil refining.'

Bevan and Calder glanced at one another, their expressions displaying incomprehension.

'I have long been an opponent of drilling for oil in

the Arctic Ocean,' he continued, 'I have written many scientific papers on the alternatives. The problem for the oil companies is that the research involved is lengthy and there are no guaranteed results. Fortunately, Skaldic Conglomerates has funded my team for the past decade. Some of the environmentalist groups tar all oil workers with the same brush, but the larger organisations are actually very supportive of our work.'

Andy nodded. 'Did you get a good look at the man who attacked you?'

'It was very dark. I had just reached for my keys when I was grabbed from behind and shoved against the bonnet of my car. The punches came thick and fast, mostly aimed at my body but some at my face. It was one of the blows to my head that made me lose consciousness. I have to assume that the assault carried on after that time. At one point early on, I tried to twist around and noticed the man was wearing a balaclava. That was all I saw.'

'Did you ever have a theory as to who was responsible?' Dani asked.

Holm smiled wryly. 'I actually always assumed it was a case of mistaken identity. I couldn't imagine who would want to harm me in that way.'

The two detectives stood up and thanked the scientist for his time. As they approached the door, Andy turned back and said, 'who had you been having dinner with - if you don't mind me asking?'

Holm looked firstly confused and then he caught Calder's drift. 'Oh, it was an office party. The attack took place in December and we were at the restaurant for our Christmas meal.'

'Thank you Mr Holm,' Andy replied. 'I hope we won't have to bother you again.'

Chapter Seventeen

The car hadn't returned, as far as Bill could tell. He tried to ring DCI Bevan at her office to give her the registration number to run a check, but was told she was out of the country on an investigation. He and Joy assumed it must be related to a new lead in the Maisie Riddell case. Bill wondered if she'd gone to Norway, as that was where the father now lived. There'd certainly been no more mention of the girl on the news. Soon she would become just another forgotten teenage runaway, unless the police found a body, of course.

Over breakfast, Bill recalled another detective that Bevan had often talked about, he had to look after his daughters and remained in Glasgow if his colleagues were following a lead which took them out of town. He knew Andy Calder would be with his boss, but he considered giving this Sergeant Boag a try. Once he'd filled the dishwasher, Bill retrieved the Pitt Street number and called the switchboard once again. This time, he was transferred to the Serious Crime Division. It was Phil Boag himself who answered. The Detective Sergeant appeared to have heard of Bill and he patiently listened to his account of the mysterious car parked opposite their house overnight.

'Do you have any reason to believe someone might wish to cause you or your wife harm?'

Bill hesitated for a moment. 'Well, I've been doing a little digging into the Stonehaven murder case. DCI Bevan may have mentioned that I have an interest in it. Perhaps my actions have been noted by somebody.'

Phil sighed. 'If you give me the registration of the car I'll run it through the system. My guess is it could be the eastern division. If you've been poking around their case you might find you've been put on a suspect list. It would be a good idea for me to have a word with them anyway, so they don't waste time and money on surveillance. I'm sure DCI Bevan has already told you this, Bill, but you really must steer clear of police matters.'

'She did say something to that effect, yes. Could you just let me know what you manage to find out about the vehicle, Sergeant Boag? Then I promise that will be an end to it.'

*

Dieter Karlsen was waiting for the Scottish detectives when they returned to their hotel. He asked if they would like to have a drink with him in the bar. They chose a semi-circular booth by the tall windows, beyond which was nothing but blackness.

'How was Aron?' Dieter enquired, eyeing Dani over the top of his beer.

'He wasn't overjoyed about having to discuss the incident again, but he was very helpful. He seems like a decent guy.'

'Aron has always been a very good boss to Sofie. She admires him and feels privileged to play a part in his work.'

Andy polished off his bottle of lager and stood up. 'I'm going to my room, Ma'am. I promised to call Carol before eight.'

'Of course,' Dani responded quickly. 'I'll see you at breakfast.'

When Andy had gone, the Norwegian asked, 'is your husband a policeman too?'

Dani smiled. 'I'm not married. I have a partner who is also a detective, but the situation is complicated. We don't get to see one another very often.'

Dieter nodded. 'It is always complicated for us. Sofie doesn't always understand my job and she feels I don't show enough interest in hers.'

'Do you have children?' Dani took a sip of her mineral water, trying to assess the man's mood.

'Yes. Our son is fourteen. His name is Christof.' Dieter ran a hand down his thigh. 'I apologise for not mentioning the Holm case sooner. Magda had said we should, but I felt it wasn't connected to the Riddells.'

'I think you're probably right,' was all Dani replied, not wishing to sour relations with their Norwegian hosts. They would get nowhere with the investigation without the assistance of the local bureau.

'You suggested that your wife had received threats before. Do you know which groups sent them to her?'

Dieter threw up his hands in a gesture of defeat. 'We have received some at home, but not for at least a year. I have them all tested for fingerprints and handwriting. We've never been able to find out who sent them.'

'It seems strange, as Holm told us his research will mean there is no need to drill in the Arctic. I would have thought his department would be heroes to the environmentalists.'

Dieter grimaced. 'Groups like Greenpeace and Save the Oceans understand the complexities of the situation. The smaller pressure groups simply get hold of a list of names and addresses and fire out hate mail. The internet has been a Godsend to them. Before now, we had never seen these people as a threat, just an irritant. I'm still not sure they are.'

Dani edged forward, as an idea came to her. 'Was your wife at the restaurant on the night that Aron Holm was attacked?'

'Yes, she was. We interviewed everyone who'd attended the meal. Nobody saw what happened after Aron left.'

Bevan nodded, slowly considering this. 'Could I take a look at the statements in the morning? Perhaps Magda would translate them for me?'

'Of course, although I'm not sure what you hope to find.' Within an instant, the detective had shifted around the bench so that their thighs were touching. At this close proximity Dani could feel the warmth from his beery breath on her cheek.

The movement was enough to give the DCI a warning of what was to come. She shifted her jacket onto her lap and slid away from him fractionally, stiffening her posture.

'Okay, I get the message,' he said quietly, standing up to leave. Dieter paused for a moment and then leant down to place a soft, stubbly kiss on her lips. He straightened back up and walked out of the hotel, leaving Dani totally bemused and with her heart pounding fiercely inside her chest.

Chapter Eighteen

Dani Bevan cleared her throat as she poured out two coffees from the pot. 'After you left last night, Dieter kind of made a pass at me.'

Andy paused, with a spoonful of muesli poised half-way to his mouth. He rested it back in the bowl. 'Sorry, I shouldn't have left you alone with him.'

'It isn't your fault. I could handle it perfectly well. I'm only mentioning the incident at all because I thought his timing was odd.'

'What do you mean?'

'Well, I'd never sensed that Karlsen was attracted to me before. His approach felt a little contrived to be honest, like he was doing it for another reason entirely.'

Andy cracked a wry smile. 'He must have fancied you one hell of a lot to try it on while you were wearing *that*.' He tipped his head towards Dani's oversized roll-neck sweater.

Bevan chuckled. 'Cheers pal, you don't look much better yourself.' Andy had swapped the snowflake jumper of the previous day for one sporting festive bands of galloping reindeer. 'I think he was attempting to divert me from this Aron Holm case. I'd just asked to see the witness statements when he started sidling up to me. I got the distinct feeling he didn't want us to probe into it any further.'

Andy lifted the coffee cup to his lips. 'Then let's make sure it's the very first thing we do when we get to the office.'

*

If Karlsen was embarrassed about what had happened the previous evening, he showed no sign of it as the two Brits joined his investigation team that morning. Magda had already dug out the files for them. She pulled up a seat for Dani so they could examine the statements together. What Bevan immediately noticed about the transcripts was how brief they were. It didn't take Magda long to run through the key facts whilst Dani jotted down notes.

'There were nine people in the restaurant on the evening that Holm was assaulted. According to these statements, he'd been acting perfectly normally throughout the meal. Holm left a little earlier than the majority of the group, although two others also departed at a similar time. This pair, a man and a woman, left through the front entrance and didn't see Aron again. Holm exited out of a side door, which led into the street where his car was parked.

Because of the limited evidence, we decided it was simply a random attack. Holm carried his wallet in the top pocket of his shirt. As the evening of the assault was so cold, he was wearing many layers over the top of it. His assailant hadn't a hope of easily finding it on his person,' Magda explained.

'But the attacker never asked him for it. According to Holm, the man didn't utter a single word. I would expect a mugger to demand money with menaces, not just beat the guy up for the heck of it.'

Magda's cheeks flushed pink. 'Don't you ever have violent attacks on the streets of Glasgow? From what we hear on the news, I believe that you certainly do.' The detective began collecting together the papers and stuffing them angrily into the file.

Dani knew they most definitely did have a

problem with violence in Glasgow, but she also knew there was always a pattern to it - some kind of weird logic. If folk got beaten up in bar brawls, they were usually pie-eyed on booze. You might get stabbed for trying to break up a fight or threatened with a kicking in front of a cash machine. But Bevan couldn't identify this type of circumstance in Holm's case. That's why it wasn't sitting well with her. For now, there wasn't much more she could do about it.

Andy strode across the room to join them. 'I've managed to extract the details of the two companies vying for the Barents Oil contract. Should we pay Riddell a visit and see if we can find out some more?'

Dani didn't need any further encouragement to get out of the bureau. She lifted her jacket and guided Calder towards the door.

*

The detectives had borrowed a squad car to reach the Riddells' property, which lay in the middle of a forest on the outskirts of the town. As they bumped along the stoney track, Dani was reminded of those Germanic fairy tales you got told as a child. When the property finally came into view, with its hardwood cladding and single story design, it made Dani think of Little Red Riding Hood's cabin in the woods and was immediately glad that she lived in the centre of a bustling city.

Dani spent a few moments examining the front of the property, noting where the pram had been left by Charlie's wife, trying to work out where someone might have hidden themselves from view until the woman had disappeared inside. Calder rang the bell. It was Charles Riddell who answered. He looked much better than when they last saw him.

'Any news on Maisie?' The man immediately asked, before they had even stepped over the threshold. Bevan noted with a heavy-heart how the light of hope still shone brightly in his tired eyes.

'I'm afraid not. Our team in Glasgow is working very hard to trace her whereabouts but we've had no response to our appeals.'

Charlie hung his head and led them into a vast, open-plan living and kitchen area. A bank of windows faced a lawned area which ended after about a hundred feet, at a thick line of pine trees. Bevan didn't much rate the view, it made her involuntarily shiver.

The Riddells' infant, Gabriel, was crawling happily along a rug in front of a wood-burning stove which was unlit. A thin woman with straight blond hair sat on the sofa in front of the child, grasping a wooden rattle in her hands.

'This is my wife, Kristin, and our little boy. As you can see, he is totally unaffected by his ordeal. We, on the other hand, have been quite badly shaken up.' Charles placed a kettle on the stove.

The police officers sat on the sofa opposite Kristin. Dani noticed how her eyes were the most perfect sky blue.

'Do you know who did this to us yet?' She asked.

It suddenly struck Bevan that the woman seated before them was probably most men's idea of the epitome of beauty. She promptly shook the idea out of her head. 'We are currently working on several leads, but we do not have a suspect.'

Kristin sighed heavily. 'Are we safe here? Should I take Gabe to my mother's house?'

'Has anything else happened to make you fearful?' Calder enquired. 'Have you seen anyone hanging around the property or received any threats?'

'We would have informed you straight away if we had,' Charlie commented, as he set down their coffee cups on a low table of typically Scandinavian design.

'I seriously doubt that this person will come near the house again,' Bevan said in a level voice. 'The police have been here on a regular basis since Gabriel was moved. This was an opportunist attack, I'm quite sure of it. Whoever did this won't be back.'

Kristin nodded and made direct eye contact with Dani. The DCI's words seemed to have reassured her. 'I'm glad to hear you say that. Charlie has been suggesting the same thing, but I needed to be told by someone in authority.'

Bevan turned towards Maisie's father. 'We don't believe that an environmental group is responsible for taking your son. Can you think of another party who might have reason to put pressure on you? We noticed that your company is in the process of handing out contracts to drilling companies. It must be a very competitive business.'

Charles put a hand up to his chin and rubbed at it. 'Yes, but the final decision has very little to do with me. These projects are part funded by the Norwegian government. The ultimate decision about which companies we use out in the Arctic has to be passed through parliament itself. I even think that there's an EU committee who need to sign off on it, as Norway is part of some European energy consortium.'

'But your recommendation must mean something?' Calder pressed.

'Yes, Emrik and I will make our preference clear in the report, although, our wishes have been ignored in the past. The politicians often have their own agendas. Barents Oil actually wants the best engineers to do the job – the ones with the spotless safety records and who treat their workers well. Not all business people are bastards. In all my time working in the oil industry, I've never once been blackmailed or intimidated. If I was, I would go straight to the authorities. Many lives are at stake out on those rigs, we don't take that responsibility lightly.'

Bevan examined the man's face closely, she was inclined to believe him. 'Have you ever heard of Aron Holm?'

Charles sat up straight and looked at her in puzzlement. 'Yes. He's the Chief Scientific Officer over at SC. Apparently, he's an absolute genius. In a few decades, the whole world will be running on synthetic oils. I've certainly read his papers on the subject.'

'Do you think he'll manage to pull it off?' Andy asked, genuinely interested.

'It might surprise you to hear that I really hope so. Holm's processes still require crude oil, just in far smaller quantities than we currently use. The world's oil supplies will eventually run out Detective, we need to have some kind of alternative plan up our sleeves.'

'Do all of your colleagues in the oil industry feel the same way about Holm's work? He must have ruffled a few feathers with his research,' Bevan continued.

Riddell shrugged his shoulders. 'He's dismissed as an eccentric by many of the scientists at Barents. The general opinion is that Skaldic Conglomerates are taking a gamble by funding his project; most likely it will come to nothing, but if it pays off,' the man puffed out his cheeks. 'Well, they've struck gold, haven't they?'

Charles led the two detectives towards the front door. 'Hang on, wasn't Aron Holm badly assaulted a few years back? Is that why you're asking about him now – do you think there may be some kind of connection to what's happening to me and my family?'

Bevan stopped walking and turned to face him. 'We're just trying to examine every possible angle, Mr Riddell. If there's any hope of tracking your daughter down and finding out who snatched your son, then I'm afraid we're going to have to.'

Chapter Nineteen

'She's very beautiful,' Dani said absent-mindedly, as they drove back towards Stavanger.

'Kristin Riddell, you mean?' Andy replied, keeping his eyes fixed on the winding road ahead. 'If she gained about 10lbs, maybe. She's too brittle to be beautiful. I prefer something soft to hold onto.'

'Too much information, thanks,' Dani said, with a smile on her lips. She thought about Carol Calder, who was every bit as pretty as Kristin but probably a couple of stone heavier. 'Is she the kind of woman that men commit crimes for?'

Andy shifted round to look at his boss. 'Not this man, but I get your point. There might be plenty who would. Where are you going with this, Ma'am?'

'I'm not sure, just thinking out loud, really.'

'Kristin is obviously more tolerant of Charles' working patterns. What Fiona found impossible to live with, she has accepted.'

'It appears that way, although we can never know what's really going on in a relationship. I can't imagine anyone being happy in that house, stuck out in the middle of nowhere. Kristin and the baby must be there a great deal by themselves. It's very isolated.'

'That's what many people crave,' Andy added sagely. 'But the Riddell's peace has been shattered now. The idea that a person has been on their property, watching the family, able to take the baby from under their noses, whatever we might say to reassure them, it will have ruined everything.'

*

Dieter Karlsen was waiting for Bevan and Calder when they got back to the Bureau. 'You've had a telephone message from Sergeant Boag,' he informed them. 'He wants you to call him as soon as possible.'

Bevan glanced at her watch. 'Is it to do with the Maisie Riddell case?'

'He said not,' Dieter replied. 'Phil gave me an update. There are no further leads at his end.'

Bevan nodded. 'Okay then, I'll ring him later.'

'Did you get much out of Charles Riddell?'

'I really don't believe he's being intimidated or blackmailed by anybody. The man is desperate to get his daughter back. I genuinely think he'd tell us if he was.'

'I've put Magda onto the job of checking his phone records; at home and work. If he's been in contact with an organisation that he shouldn't have, we'll soon find out.'

Dani asked Andy to help Magda with this line of enquiry, telling him she needed to pop out for a while. Bevan ignored the suspicious look that Dieter shot her when she scooped up the keys to a squad car and marched out of the bureau.

The DCI was headed into the older quarter of Stavanger, back to the office building of Skaldic Conglomerates. She had no appointment and no authority to question witnesses, so Dani simply hoped that the person she was here to see would be cooperative. Bevan showed her badge to the receptionist and was told to wait at a seating area in the lobby. Eventually, a dark-haired woman of a similar age to herself; dressed in a figure-hugging sweater and woollen skirt, stepped out of the lift. Dani knew immediately that this was Sofie Karlsen.

Bevan stood up and put out her hand. 'Mrs

Karlsen. Thank you so much for giving up your time to speak with me.'

The scientist managed a thin smile. 'I'm on a break. Can we go out and buy a coffee somewhere?'

'Of course.'

Pleased to finally get the chance to see something of Stavanger itself, Dani allowed Sofie to lead her into a quaint little tea-shop that overlooked a market square of 18th Century buildings. They both ordered strong coffees and a plate of tiny pastries.

'I've no right to ask you questions, I realise that. But we are in the middle of a missing persons inquiry – a young Scottish girl, just fourteen years old, hasn't been seen for several days now. Her father works at Barents Oil. I think her disappearance may be connected to the attack on your boss, Aron Holm.'

'She's the same age as our son,' Sofie said quietly, sipping the jet black liquid.

'Then you'll understand how distraught her parents are. The longer Maisie is away from home, the more it will seem as if she is just another teenage runaway. I believe there is more to it than that.' Bevan watched the woman's pretty face closely.

'You mustn't waste any more time on Aron's case. It has nothing to do with your missing girl.'

'I realise that the Criminal Investigation Service has decided it was a random attack, but the evidence just doesn't fit that explanation. As soon as I read the details I knew it was planned – this man was targeted. He was attacked in an area without CCTV coverage and with a broken street light. You were dining in the restaurant that evening. Are you certain you saw nothing suspicious?' Bevan leant forward, so that her arms were resting on the table and their hands were nearly touching.

Sofie let out a tiny sigh. 'Can I not persuade you

to let the issue drop? If I tell you what I know, we will lose everything.' The green of the woman's eyes had begun to mist and swirl with tears.

'I have no jurisdiction here in Norway. If you satisfy me that this case has nothing to do with my investigation, then my colleague and I will go back to Scotland. It will be none of our business.'

Sofie breathed in a sob. 'I have a friend. He works with me. His name is Jakob and I love him very much. Dieter and I have been experiencing problems for many years. He is hardly ever at home. I needed someone to care for me, to cherish me. I thought that Dieter knew about my friendship and never for one moment did I imagine that he would care.

But it turned out he did. Dieter was watching us. He'd been doing it for months. When the evening of our office party came around, he followed Jakob to the restaurant. My lover got a lift there with Aron, because he wanted to be able to have a drink. But I was going to drive him back home again, so we left out of the front exit, a little after our boss did.

Dieter was waiting down that side alley. I think he'd been driven half-mad by his jealousy. The only way he could communicate with me by that stage was by seeing me as part of one of his precious cases – by observing me from an unmarked car on a dark street corner. When poor Aron came out of the restaurant door, because he was all wrapped up in winter clothes, Dieter thought it was Jakob. He vented all his anger and frustration through his fists, beating the man senseless. As soon as I heard what had happened I just knew it had been my husband who was responsible. Dieter told me everything, once he realised the terrible mistake he had made.'

'Does anybody else know about this?'

'I think Magda Hustad suspects it, but she would

never say. She is devoted to Dieter.' Tears as round as little glass ornaments were sliding down her face, reflecting back the lights of the café. 'I never wanted our son to find out.'

'Thank you for allowing me to have coffee with you. Please stay here whilst I pay. Take some time to compose yourself before returning to the office.' Dani laid her hand briefly on top of Sofie's, left a few notes on the counter top and stepped out into the street.

Conflicting thoughts were bombarding the DCI as she strode back to the squad car. She sat in the front seat for several minutes, doing absolutely nothing. Then Dani jolted into action, taking the mobile phone out of her pocket and placing a call to Phil Boag's desk at the Pitt Street Headquarters in Glasgow. Her Sergeant answered swiftly, launching into a diatribe she had to struggle to keep up with. What Bevan managed to pick out of the jumble of words, was that Phil had mentioned a name she'd not heard in a while. The sound of it now, in this distant town in a faraway land, sent shivers of fear and dread shooting down her spine.

Richard Erskine.

Chapter Twenty

Bevan was trying to adjust her mind to accommodate the sight of Bill and Joy Hutchison, sitting stiffly upright, on the sofa of her office in the Serious Crime Division of Police Scotland. She'd not seen the couple in several months and they looked entirely unchanged.

Dani stood with Andy Calder by Phil's desk, peering at their guests through the glass partition, like a group of gawping children outside the tiger enclosure at Glasgow Zoo. 'So, Richard Erskine's car was parked opposite the Hutchisons' house all night and Bill thinks the man was in the front seat watching them.'

'Bill noted down the registration number. When I had a spare moment, I ran it through the system. The car was registered to Erskine at his Inverness address,' Phil clarified.

'Why is Richard Erskine interested in the Hutchisons?' Andy looked utterly incredulous.

'That's what I intend to find out.' Dani paced across the floor. Taking a deep breath, she walked purposefully into the office.

Bill leapt to his feet. 'Detective Chief Inspector! How lovely to see you. Did you enjoy your trip to Norway?'

Dani was immediately wrong-footed, certain that Phil would never have disclosed where she and Andy had been for the last few days. She simply ignored the comment and ploughed on, 'yes, it is good to see you both. I just wish it was under different circumstances.'

Bill looked sheepish. 'I know you told me to leave the investigating to the authorities, but I just had this one lead. I thought if I could chase it up, I'd leave things at that.'

Dani sat down in the seat opposite them. 'So you visited this 'Fisherman's Bar' in Aberdeen. Did you pick up anything useful while you were there?'

'I met a few of Sinclair's drinking pals. One of them, who referred to himself as Stewart, seemed to think that Sinclair was involved in illegal activities of some sort – I got the impression it was to do with buying and selling.'

'I'll give DI Lyons a call and run the information by him. His team may already be aware of all this.'

Joy nudged Bill's arm gently. 'There was something else too, wasn't there dear?'

Bill was hesitant. 'It was more of a *feeling* than a solid piece of evidence. I told Joy about it afterwards, because I'd left the place with a sense of uneasiness.'

Dani nodded encouragingly, knowing that despite appearances, Bill's instincts were finely-tuned.

'There was a young girl working out in the kitchens. I only caught the vaguest glimpse of her, but when I did, the situation struck me as odd. She was very young, fifteen at the most, I'd say. Her colouring was so fair that you might even have thought she was albino. When I asked the manageress about the girl, her attitude immediately changed, in a way I couldn't quite put my finger on - as if she were reassessing me, perhaps.'

Dani sat back and considered this for a moment. 'Did anyone see you enter the bar, or follow you to Aberdeen?'

Bill shook his head. 'The road was practically empty. Most cars were driving *out* of the city at that time on a Friday evening.'

'Okay. I'll speak with DI Lyons first thing in the

morning. You say that Erskine's car hasn't been back since?'

'No,' said Joy. 'I think he knows we spotted him.'

'I'll get the Falkirk station to send a squad car down your road every couple of hours just in case, but I think you're right. If it was Erskine in that car, he'll not be back in a hurry. He's a very clever man, not one to slip up twice.'

Bill shuffled forward in the seat, lowering his voice unnecessarily. 'What interest can Erskine have in us? How did the man discover I had my suspicions about him being responsible for Sinclair's murder?'

'I don't know Bill, but Erskine isn't superhuman. There must be some kind of logical reason why he's turned his attention to you. But don't worry, I'll find out what it is.'

When Dani returned to her flat she was completely exhausted. After kicking off her shoes, she dropped her case in the hallway and left it there, padding straight into the kitchen-diner. Bevan had a series of messages on her answering machine, so she brewed a pot of tea and sat at the table to listen to them, gently massaging her foot as she did so.

A couple were from her father in Colonsay. They described the fairly mundane routines of a fortnight's worth of island life, which to Dani sounded utterly blissful. Another was from Sam Sharpe, her American boyfriend. He knew she was in the midst of a case and wouldn't expect a reply. The final message was from Fiona Riddell. Her voice sounded oddly distant. She was ringing for an update on what they'd found out in Norway. Dani took a quick sip of tea and fished out her mobile phone, knowing that this was a call she'd certainly have to return.

*

Dani had met DI Lyons once at a function. She knew that he was mid-fifties and not far off retirement. He was also a perfectly pleasant man and had seemed dedicated to the job. When Dani had run through the information she'd gleaned from the Hutchisons, she gave the man a few moments to respond.

'Well, you realise this is highly irregular, DCI Bevan - to have a civilian running around town, interfering in a live murder inquiry. We could easily have a court injunction slapped on the fella.'

'Mr Hutchison has sworn to me that he will stop his investigations now. I don't think that it will be necessary to take things any further.'

Lyons grunted.

'It is strange, don't you think, that Erskine has been watching the Hutchisons' house. If the man has got nothing to do with Sinclair's murder, why is he so interested in Bill?'

'Perhaps because Hutchison has been busily slandering his name the length and breadth of Scotland. In the eyes of the law, Erskine is an innocent man. He's been tried and found not guilty of any crime, yet Bill Hutchison is trying to label him a serial killer.'

'But how would Erskine know what Bill's been saying? He's only voiced his suspicions to the police. *I* certainly haven't mentioned it to anybody outside the force.'

'I hope you aren't suggesting that one of my team has let the information leak, Detective Chief Inspector? I hear this Hutchison chap's not quite the full ticket. If there's been any loose talk, I bet it's come from him.'

Dani wondered who DI Lyons had been discussing the Hutchisons with. 'Where are you at with the Sinclair case, Ian? Were you aware that your victim was a petty criminal who's been operating around the Aberdeen area for decades?'

'We know Sinclair was arrested a couple of times in connection with smuggling out of Aberdeen Harbour. This is our main line of inquiry at present. A couple of his ex-bosses can't give us an alibi for the night the man was killed. It's just a question now of trying to get the forensics to tie one of them into the scene. There was so much blood. It'll just be a matter of time.'

But the blood would have been all Sinclair's, Dani thought to herself, remembering the Mackie Shaw case and how the man was attacked from behind, the blood from the severed arteries in his neck spurting out onto the wall of the shed. Unless they could find the assailant's clothing, they wouldn't be able to get a forensic match. 'Erskine makes sure he takes a change of clothing with him. He knows that the scene is going to get messy. If you can find those clothes, or the place where they were disposed of, then you'll have got your man, bang to rights.'

There was silence on the line for several seconds. Dani wondered if the inspector was still there. 'I'll take that under advisement,' he said finally.

'Do you know much about what goes on at the Fisherman's Bar? There have been a few raids in relation to smuggling and the fencing of stolen goods, but do you know of any connection to the employment of underage girls, possibly of eastern European origin?'

'I'd have to get onto Vice and check it out with them.'

'Be sure to do that for me would you, Inspector? And let me know what you find out by the end of play today.'

Chapter Twenty One

Detective Sergeant Boag led the briefing, explaining to the team how Bevan and Calder's trip to Norway tied into their investigation back at home.

'I'm not prepared to rule out the involvement of some kind of extremist group in the disappearance of Maisie, even if it is just a rogue individual,' Dani explained as a postscript. 'Although, I believe we should discount the assault on Aron Holm. I'm certain there's no connection between that and our case.'

Phil nodded. 'We'll take your word for it, Ma'am.'

DC Mann stepped forward. 'In the last couple of days, I've widened out the area of our search. I was assuming that Maisie Riddell could have travelled some considerable distance by this time, particularly if she is being assisted by someone who has a vehicle.'

'Have you come up with anything, Alice?'

'I got a call this morning from a detective in Newcastle, I've not had the chance to follow it up properly yet. He thinks there may have been a sighting there.'

Bevan's body tensed up. 'Get back to them straight away. If you think the evidence is strong enough, take another member of the team and get yourself down to Northumberland today.'

*

The Port of Tyne was gloomy, even though it was only three in the afternoon. A kind of damp mist was rolling in off the iron-grey sea. DC Alice Mann and DC Dan Clifton were there to see the owner of one of the shipping companies that operated from out of the Dock. His office was in a single-story prefab, nestled within a row of enormous containers.

Rick Wilshaw opened the door to them and led the detectives inside. The man's face was virtually covered in a thick, dark beard, but judging by the lines criss-crossing his forehead, Alice thought he was probably late forties.

'I've been taking a shipment to Amsterdam. I only got back yesterday evening and saw the e-fits of the missing girl; they're plastered all over the passenger terminal buildings. Otherwise, I would have called the cops sooner.'

'Could you run through with us what you told the detectives at Newcastle?' Alice took a seat on a plastic chair and got out her notebook.

Wilshaw scratched vigorously at his bristly beard. 'It would have been last Thursday evening, because we set sail for Amsterdam the following day. A young man turned up here at the cabin. He was dark in colouring and I couldn't make out his accent, but I did assume he was north-east. The man wanted me to add some extra cargo to my ship. It happens quite often, I'm afraid. He offered me £2,000 cash to ship a group of people across, including himself. I told him that I operate a totally legal business here and he'd best head off quick before I called the police.'

'Did he give you his name?' Dan asked.

'No, he scarpered pretty sharpish after that. But I watched him leave from out of the window. I've got powerful lights on the front of the office and I saw his little rag-tag group standing out there on the concrete.'

'How many where there?'

'About fifteen, perhaps. What stuck in my mind was that there were women amongst them, some really quite young. But one girl looked different from the others. She was dressed in the kind of clothes that my daughter would wear. When I saw the photograph, it immediately occurred to me that it could very well have been that missing girl. She had dark, shoulder-length hair and those sad eyes.'

'And you've no idea where this group went to next?' Alice stopped writing and looked directly at Wilshaw.

'I expect they tried the other shipping companies along this dock. I don't think any of them would have taken the group aboard, but you never know, do you? I've done this job for twenty years and nothing surprises me now.'

'Why do you think these people were trying to get to Amsterdam?' Dan enquired, interested in the man's opinion on this.

'They're usually illegals. The government's clamping down on them more heavily these days. If their visas have expired and they want to avoid being deported to some warzone, then they'll try to move about Europe. There's always work to be had, especially in the industrial areas of Denmark and Germany.'

The detectives divided the port up between them and began asking around the different shipping companies that operated there. As they had suspected, absolutely no one was admitting to taking this particular group of illegal immigrants across to Holland. One other man had remembered them, he too was surprised by the presence of women in the group, but he gave the detectives less information than Wilshaw had.

After a couple of hours, Alice led the way back to the car. 'I suppose the evidence is fairly flimsy. We've only got Wilshaw's identification, on a dark, foggy night, from the dirty window of his pre-fab.'

'Aye, it wouldn't stand up in court,' Clifton replied, climbing into the driver's seat. 'But I thought the guy was believable. I think it's very possible he saw Maisie, the timing certainly fits. She would have been here about 24 hours after she stepped out of the school building in Glasgow.'

Dan manoeuvred the vehicle out through a gate in the tall, metal fence that encircled the port. Alice glanced across at the ferry terminal, where enormous ships were docked for the night and others were ploughing through the rough seas, piercingly bright lights fixed to their bows.

'Pull up a bit closer to the terminal building will you?' She suddenly asked, leaning forward to read the neon information sign which was displaying a rolling commentary of weather conditions and potential delays. 'Have you ever heard of a place called Kristiansand? It's one of the destinations on that board.'

Dan shook his head. 'Try Googling it on your phone.'

Alice carefully tapped the letters into a search engine. Within seconds, she had a result. 'I think this might be significant, Dan. It's in Vest Agder, Norway.'

*

Bevan noticed her mobile phone bleeping as she got out of the car. She reached into her bag and carefully read the text message from Alice Mann as she stood at the end of her front garden. Dani put out a hand without looking and absent-mindedly pushed open the wrought-iron gate, which creaked as it moved. It was the only sound to be heard on her residential street this late at night. With her eyes still fixed on the screen, she reached the front door, only then shifting her gaze upwards. As she did so, a figure lunged from out of the shadows, clamping a hand over her mouth and pulling her roughly into the darkness.

Chapter Twenty Two

'I need to speak to you. Can I come in?'

'Dieter? Christ! You scared the life out of me.' Once released from his grip Dani brushed down her jacket and reached for her house keys.

'I'm sorry, but I couldn't leave things the way they were. Will you talk to me?'

'Of course, come inside, before one of my neighbours calls the police,' she added with irony.

Bevan flicked on the lights as they entered, leading the Norwegian straight into the kitchen at the rear of the property. 'I'm going to make some coffee. I suspect we'll need to keep clear heads.'

Dieter nodded, sitting down at the table. His stubble was even thicker and his eyes were bloodshot. 'You and Calder left so quickly. I didn't know what to think.'

Dani turned to face him, resting her weight against the counter. 'Have you spoken to Sofie?'

He raised pleading eyes in her direction. 'Yes. She told me about your conversation. *Please* Dani, I need to know what you are going to do with the information. I am going mad with worry.'

'There's nothing I *can* do. I had absolutely no authority to speak with Sofie. If the case ever went to court I expect she'd deny the conversation took place. Besides that, I'm not sure what good it would do for you to lose your job and go to prison.' Dani busied herself making a pot of coffee. 'Although, if you go on to kill your wife's lover at some stage in the future, I expect I'll learn to regret my decision.'

Dieter was suddenly by her side. 'I would never

do that. It might surprise you to know I'm not a violent person. When I attacked Aron Holm I was not well. My marriage was in tatters, I'd tortured myself for weeks by watching Sofie fall in love with another man. I won't be able to forgive myself for my actions, but I might be able to make amends through my police work. I *am* a good detective.'

'I know you are.' Dani allowed him to slide his arm around her waist and bury his face into her neck. 'Look, you really don't need to seduce me in order to ensure my silence. I've already made my decision. You aren't that irresistible, Dieter.'

He immediately lifted his head up, a surprised expression on his face. 'That is not what I'm doing.'

'It's late. I'll get you a duvet and pillow. The sofa is actually quite comfortable. Take the pot of coffee through into the front room and go to sleep whenever you like.'

Dieter leant forward and placed that gentle kiss on her lips once again. 'You are a good woman,' he muttered.

'I'm a bloody saint,' she replied with a smile, withdrawing herself from his embrace and going to fetch the spare bedding.

*

When Dani got up the next morning, Dieter was making pancakes at her stove. She couldn't remember the last time she'd used the appliance herself.

'Where on earth did you find the ingredients for that?' She said in genuine disbelief.

'You had some eggs and milk in the fridge and a half packet of flour in a cupboard. It was a little out-of-date, but still.'

'I think there's a jar of honey too. No syrup though, I'm afraid.' Dani set the table and made some tea.

Dieter brought a plate of steaming pancakes over. He seemed less jittery than he was the previous night.

'If you were going to travel from the UK to Norway, what routes could you use?' Dani suddenly asked.

'I flew from Stavanger to Glasgow yesterday, as you and Andy would have done. The quickest flight to Scotland is via Aberdeen. But you can fly to most British airports from Oslo these days.'

'What about travelling by sea?' Dani lifted a mug of tea to her lips.

Dieter smiled. 'A long and unpleasant voyage, I would expect.' Then, sensing she was actually quite serious he continued, 'I think you can get a ferry from Newcastle or Harwich, although I'm not sure for how much longer these routes can survive, with the convenience of air travel.'

'But if you didn't have the correct travel documents, or were an illegal immigrant?'

'I thought that your Channel Tunnel was the preferred route for those kinds of people.'

'Say you wanted to reach Norway specifically and had no passport?'

'Are you talking about Maisie Riddell?' He slowly chewed a mouthful of pancake and honey.

'We may have had a sighting of her trying to travel illegally out of Newcastle. One of my officers noticed that ferries leave the Port of Tyne headed for Kristiansand.'

'That's still a long way from Stavanger. If Maisie has got caught up with people traffickers and illegals then you may never find her again. You do realise that?'

Dani nodded sadly. 'If she was still in this country we may have had a chance.'

'This identification is not absolutely certain,

114

though, is it?'

'No, and we haven't got any corroboration yet.'

'Then let's hope to God that your witness was wrong.'

Dani said nothing, finishing her tea in silence. At first she'd been excited about this possible sighting but now the DCI was beginning to think she agreed with Dieter. Once Maisie was absorbed into the underground world of organised crime in mainland Europe, their chances of finding her were incredibly slim.

Chapter Twenty Three

Fiona Riddell occupied a desk at the far end of the Sales floor of Harding Electronics. She appeared to have four young salespeople in her team. As Dani approached, the woman stood and put out her hand. Fiona was looking thinner, but she had some colour to her cheeks and managed a smile.

'Please take a seat. Sam will bring us a coffee.'

A casually dressed man of about twenty nodded his head and scuttled off into a side room.

Dani leant forward and lightly touched Fiona's hand. 'I have some news, but it's not much, I'm afraid.' She described the possible sighting of Maisie at Newcastle Docks.

Fiona gave out a huge sigh which could also have been a sob. 'So she might still be alive? If she managed to get on a boat headed somewhere.'

'This sighting was the day after her disappearance. It was over a week ago. We don't know what's become of her since.' Dani knew she had to manage Fiona's expectations, to keep the poor woman realistic about what might have happened to her daughter.

'Okay.' She nodded vigorously but her eyes were filled with tears of relief. 'Where would she have been going? Why would Maisie want to reach Amsterdam?'

Dani chose her words carefully. 'If she were going to Amsterdam, it may have been in order to find work - the type of work which doesn't require the correct documentation.'

Fiona's hand shot up to her face, as she realised

the implications of this. 'Oh my God! Could there be another reason?' The woman's eyes were pleading with her.

'Yes. Our experts say that pretty much the only way to reach Norway now by sea is to go to Holland or Denmark and make your way from there. Amsterdam may very well not have been Maisie's final destination. She didn't have her passport with her so she couldn't have taken a plane.'

'You think she may have been going to find her father? But why all the subterfuge?'

Dani shook her head. 'I don't know yet. But if this is the route she chose, Maisie must have had connections with some very shady people who could have arranged the travel for her. Can you think of anyone out of the ordinary that your daughter had a connection with, however fleeting, in the weeks before she left?'

'I'll think about it really carefully Detective Chief Inspector,' Fiona said eagerly. Then the hopefulness that had lit up her face began to quickly fade. 'But if Maisie set off over a week ago to get to her father's place, why hasn't she reached there yet?'

'I don't know, Fiona, I just don't know.'

Bevan met Andy Calder back at the station. She waited until he had finished a phone conversation before informing him of the details of her meeting with Fiona Riddell.

Andy looked thoughtful. 'I want to have another word with Georgina Boag. If Maisie was involved with the kind of people who could smuggle a young girl out of the country, she *must* have confided in someone about it. Georgie was her best friend.'

Dani grimaced. 'Yes, I agree. But we've got to have one of her parents present, or an appropriate adult.'

'Why don't we have Jane there this time? It might be worthwhile to try something out of left field.'

'It's worth a shot,' Dani said resignedly. 'Let's give the woman a call and set up a meeting for this afternoon.'

*

On the drive to Newton High School, Andy cleared his throat and said, 'do you mind if I ask a personal question?'

'It depends on what it is,' Dani replied warily.

'Why is Dieter Karlsen staying at your flat?'

The DCI nearly spat out the sip of cappuccino she'd just taken from her cardboard cup. 'How the hell do you know about that?'

'Carol called me earlier. She was unpacking my bags for me and found some of your purchases from Duty Free in there. We'd left in such a hurry that we hadn't divided our stuff properly. Carol decided to take a walk over to your place with Amy in the pram. She was going to leave the bag down your side passage and post a note through the letterbox. When she got there, a man was coming out of your front door. Carol described him as tall, unshaven, handsome and with a Scandinavian accent.'

'Oh,' Dani said quietly.

'Is there something you're not telling me, Ma'am?'

Plenty, Dani thought to herself. 'He's taken a few weeks holiday. Dieter is having problems at home.'

'It's none of my business, obviously. But what would Sam say if he knew?'

Dani shifted around to face her partner. 'You're not going to tell him are you?'

'No, of course not. I just want you to be careful.'

'It isn't actually what you think. Dieter turned up late last night. I let him sleep on my sofa. He's welcome to stay for a few days until he sorts things

118
out.'

'I could come round and have a word; tell the guy to find a hotel. You don't want him starting to get his feet under the table.'

Dani smiled. 'I've got it covered, thanks. I hope Carol and Amy didn't get too much of a fright.'

'Apparently he invited them in for tea. He'd made some biscuits. Carol thought he was very nice and wondered where you'd been hiding him.'

'Good,' Dani said firmly. 'I'm glad he's making himself at home.'

*

Jane Boag was sitting ram-rod straight behind her desk. The police officers faced Georgina on the soft chairs in the corner of the headmistress's office. Dani was certain that the woman's overbearing presence would surely stifle any kind of response from her daughter. She was finding it rather unsettling herself.

'I realise DC Calder has spoken with you already, but we have some new information, Georgie.'

The girl lifted her large eyes towards the DCI, opening them wide. 'Do you know where she is?'

'No. But she may have been trying to reach Scandinavia, possibly to see her father. A girl matching her description was spotted trying to get on a boat going to Amsterdam.' Dani looked at the girl's face and saw only confusion. 'Maisie was with a group of people who were trying to gain passage illegally. A couple of individuals were offering a great deal of money to traffic this group to the continent. Have you any idea how your friend might have known these men?'

Georgie clutched her hands tightly in her lap, her eyes suddenly darting to and fro.

'Georgina!' boomed the headmistress. 'Do you know something about this? You must tell the

Detective Chief Inspector immediately!'

Both Dani and Andy nearly jumped out of their skins at the ferocity of the outburst. At first, the young girl before them began to rock back and forth, tears spilling down her plump, rosy cheeks. Then, she took several deep, calming breaths and finally, began to speak. 'It happened a number of times. Maisie said she needed to meet a friend in town and would I cover for her. All I had to do was tell Mrs Riddell that Maisie was at home with me if she called on those particular evenings, but she never did.'

'Can you recall the dates when this occurred?'

'Yes, I think so.'

'Did she ever tell you who she was meeting?' Andy probed gently.

'Maisie never gave me names. Although, she might have said one of the men was called Anton, or something like that. I got the sense she was working, because the hours were very precise – like 8 'till 10.30pm and I wasn't ever to call her between those times but if her mum rang then I was to stall her and tell her that Maisie would ring her back in half an hour.'

Jane Boag had moved silently across the room and placed a hand on her daughter's back. 'Why did you not tell us this before? You must realise how important it is?'

Georgie's voice became a croaky whisper. 'Because I took money to do it. Whenever I provided a cover story for Maisie, she gave me twenty pounds. I've already spent it all on clothes and stuff. I can't give it back now.' The girl gazed fearfully at Dani. 'Am I going to have to go to prison?'

Chapter Twenty Four

Bevan was reminded of her conversation with DI Lyons as she liaised with the officers of the Vice Division. Lyons had informed her the previous day that they had no record of underage girls working at the Fisherman's Bar in Aberdeen, which of course didn't mean that they weren't doing so.

Dani had brought Phil Boag along with her. She wanted to make him feel involved in this line of inquiry, sensing he was mortified about Georgina's part in facilitating Maisie's secret life.

DI Grant was running through with them what that life might have consisted of. 'Folk often assume that if a young girl is associated with the criminal underworld in Glasgow, it has to be to do with the sex trade. Mostly that's true, but there are other roles these girls can play. The hotels need serving staff and cleaners. Some kids take part in cabaret acts, not always of the seedier variety.'

'Hang on,' Dani said. 'Didn't Andy mention that Maisie sang? She had a favourite band – her and the boy next door used to perform covers of their songs.'

'I can't recall the name of it off-hand,' Phil added.

Grant nodded. 'If she had a skill set to offer, other than the obvious, Maisie might have made money that way. Or, she could have been pushing drugs for them, of course.'

'Have you got anyone on your files by the name of Anton?' Dani enquired.

'I don't need to look that up. Clive Anton. Not his real name, I'm sure. He operates in the south-east of the city, out towards Celtic Park. Clive owns several night clubs and bars. We've never been able to make a solid case against him but we know that class C drugs change hands in his establishments and probably class A. I'm certain he has illegals working for him - his staff tend to come and go.'

'Could you give us the addresses of his premises? Where are we likely to find him during the daytime?'

'I'll print you off a list,' Grant replied amiably. 'He's got a flat above one of his bars on London Road. I'd try there first.'

*

It proved tricky for Phil to find a place to park. They ended up pulling right onto the pavement, with heavy traffic whistling past their wing mirror. The pub that DI Grant had directed them to had its shutters down. There was a door next to it which seemed to give access to the residence on the first floor. Phil pressed on the bell. They heard a sash window above scrape open and saw a bald, semi-naked man leaning out into the freezing cold air. He slowly took in their appearance.

'How may I help you, Mr and Mrs Bobby?'

'Can we come up and have a word?' Phil called back, holding up his warrant card quite unnecessarily.

'What's it about?' Clive Anton rested his belly on the window frame, looking quite comfortable, despite the biting chill.

'We aren't from Vice, Mr Anton,' Dani explained. 'We're investigating the disappearance of Maisie Riddell.'

He abruptly vanished from the window. A few seconds later, the door buzzed open.

Phil led the way up the dark staircase. The internal door on the landing had been left ajar. The DS shouldered his way in. Dani had to fight an urge to put a hand up to her nose. The smell within this cramped flat was nauseating. As she glanced about her, she could see that Anton kept the place fairly clean and tidy, but the atmosphere was thick with the fumes of a sweet and sickly sort of perfume. This aroma was artificially created, but it reminded Dani of the smell that tended to linger around a decaying corpse.

'Take a seat,' Clive offered, having thankfully pulled on a shirt.

The officers perched on the edge of a purple velvet sofa. 'Do I take it you knew Maisie?' Dani asked, getting straight to the point as she wasn't sure how much longer she could remain in the place without being sick.

'She was a customer of mine,' he replied blandly, sitting on a throne-like armchair opposite them.

'A *customer*, so she didn't work for you?' Phil asked.

'Maisie was a regular down at the Basement.' When Dani looked bemused he added, 'it's one of my clubs near the centre of town. The music we play there is popular with the student types. It's not my kind of thing, but you need to give the punters what they want, eh?'

'How often did Maisie frequent your club?'

'Once or twice a month.' Clive selected a cigarette from a silver box on the table and lit up.

'Then how can you possibly remember her?' Dani asked in disbelief, whilst silently hoping that the cigarette smoke would help to neutralise the dreadful stench.

'Because she was going out with one of my DJs. Ray, his name is.'

'Can we have this man's address please,' Dani said forcefully.

'Now, I couldn't possibly give you that, but come down to the Basement tonight after ten. I believe he's doing a set.'

Dani immediately jumped up. 'We'll certainly do that, Mr Anton, thank you.'

As they made their way to the door, Phil turned back towards the man and said, 'you do realise that Maisie Riddell is only fourteen years old?'

Clive smiled broadly. 'Oh yes, Detective. That's just the age that Ray likes them.'

Chapter Twenty Five

As they stepped out into the street, Dani couldn't prevent herself from releasing a couple of dry retches.

Phil placed a hand on her back. 'I quite understand. The man made me feel physically sick, too. I don't think I could ever work Vice.'

Once they were back in the car and Dani had taken several sips from a bottle of water stashed under the seat, she recovered her composure. 'It was that awful smell in the flat. I just couldn't stomach it.'

'The perfume, you mean?' Phil replied. 'I think Sorcha's got it at home. It is a bit cloying, but we've got used to it now. All the young girls are wearing the brand. The scent is endorsed by some celebrity type.'

'It should come with a bloody health warning. What's it called, 'Eau du rotting corpse'?'

Phil chuckled. 'Clive Anton was very forthcoming about Maisie. He didn't hesitate to let us know they were acquainted.'

'As long as we can't prove he served her alcohol, employed her in his businesses or had sex with her, he's in no danger from us. I expect Clive's pretty confident that we'll never be able to find the evidence of any of those things. Vice never had in the past.'

'Bastard. Do you think this *Basement* place is where Maisie was going when Georgie gave her a cover story?'

'I think she must have done. Although Clive says she was only there once or twice a month, yet she used Georgie to provide her with an alibi more often than that.'

'Maybe this Ray chap will tell us more.' Phil glanced across sheepishly. 'I can't come out undercover with you that late. Jane's got a 'do' at the Town Hall tonight.'

'Not a problem, Phil. I wouldn't expect you to.' Dani had another plan in mind. Besides, she had absolutely no intention of getting on the wrong side of Jane Boag.

*

Dieter had dressed in dark jeans and a navy blue sweater, which clung to the contours of his muscular upper body. Dani put on the only black dress she possessed and a pair of old biker boots which she'd noticed had recently come back into fashion.

'Do we look like cops?' The Norwegian asked with a raise of his eyebrows, as they stood drinking wine in Dani's kitchen, waiting for their cab to arrive.

'Probably,' she replied with a laugh. 'We'll stick out like a sore thumb anyway, for being a couple of decades older than their usual clientele.'

'You could pass for much younger,' Dieter said quite genuinely. Dani decided for once to take it as a compliment and not as the highlighting of a professional weakness.

The taxi dropped them outside a non-descript set of double-doors, half-way along a grimy side-alley off Renfrew Street. Steep steps led them to a subterranean ticket office and cloakroom. Dani made sure that she removed all her over garments, down to her thin strappy dress, suddenly recalling the fundamentals of clubbing – very quickly she was going to get extremely hot.

The pair stood by the bar, ordering whiskies and coke. Dani vaguely recognised the thumping playlist of alternative anthems from her own student days.

'We have some places like this in Oslo, but

nothing similar in Stavanger,' Dieter hollered into her ear.

'Glasgow still has plenty of these kinds of clubs,' Dani shouted back. 'Something about them seems to appeal to us.'

They stood side by side for a while, watching the mass of sweaty bodies gyrate within the tiny dancefloor. Conversation was pretty much impossible over the music. Dani nudged Dieter's arm as the tempo of the beat subtly changed and she noticed a new DJ behind the decks. 'Let's go and have a word,' she mouthed.

The man, whom Clive Anton referred to as Ray, looked to be in his early thirties, although in the dim light it was hard to tell. Dani tapped him on the arm and flashed her warrant card. He said nothing but gestured for a younger lad to take over and led them through a door into a side room, where amps and speakers were piled up in the corner.

'My name is DCI Bevan, this is my colleague Detective Karlsen. We are part of the team investigating the disappearance of Maisie Riddell.'

The man stood up straight. In this light, Dani could see he was probably older than she'd thought. 'My name's Ray McCoughlin. How can I help you?'

'We've been informed that you were Maisie Riddell's boyfriend.'

He winced. 'I wouldn't say that. I knew her a bit, that's all.'

'Maisie came to this club a lot, did she?'

Ray shrugged his shoulders. 'Look, I never slept with her and I never got her drinks. I know she was younger than she seemed. I saw her in town with her school uniform on once. After that, I didn't use her again.'

'*Use* her?' Dieter said with emphasis, puffing himself up to his full height.

Ray lifted his hands in the air. 'Maisie sang, right? She had a really great voice. I got her doing the vocals for some bands that I work with. It was all cash in hand, I'll admit to that. When I realised she was still in school it stopped – that would have been about a month back.'

'How long had she been working for you?'

'At least a year. Maisie did really well out of it. I never exploited her.'

'Why did the person we spoke to think she was your girlfriend?' Dani stared at him hard.

'You probably won't believe me, but it was safer for her to pretend she was with me. Some of the guys who come to these places are into younger girls. Maisie would always put her arm around me if a bloke was sleazing up to her and we might snog occasionally. That was it. Maisie was a smart girl. She knew how to steer away from trouble.'

'You keep talking about her in the past tense, Ray. What do you think has happened to the girl?'

'Maisie's split, just like she always said she would when she'd saved enough cash. That girl could be anywhere by now and wherever she is she'll make it big. Maisie's got a lot of talent.'

'Did she ever tell you where she would go if she had the money?' Dieter asked.

'I was always suggesting she head to the States. Folk really appreciate her kind of voice over there. Now I think about it, Maisie never agreed or disagreed with me when I said it. She kept her cards close to her chest that one.'

'Thanks for your time,' Dani replied, feeling that she wasn't going to get much more out of him.

Before they returned to the noisy throng which lay beyond the padded door, Ray hesitated and then added, 'I've got a few recordings, if it would help.'

'I beg your pardon?'

'Of Maisie singing. They're on my phone and not of great quality. I took the videos the first time she ever performed for me. It was like a kind of audition and I used to play it to the managers of the venues I was pitching to.'

'I would like a copy of that very much, Ray.'

'Okay,' he nodded his head cockily, 'I'll see what I can do.'

*

They sat on the sofa in Dani's rarely used sitting room, the lights down low, watching the grainy image that Ray had sent to Dieter's phone.

'Maisie's voice is really beautiful,' the man said quietly.

'But it's so melancholy,' Dani muttered.

Dieter gave her a puzzled look.

'She seems so sad. Her eyes are full of misery.' To her horror, Dani found that tears were escaping onto her cheeks and a huge sob shuddered through her chest.

Dieter placed his phone down on the coffee table and pulled Dani towards him, tracing the passage of her tears with his warm lips. She allowed him to slide his hands beneath the straps of her dress and slip them off her shoulders. Dani closed her eyes as Dieter's lips reached her mouth, knowing she should be putting a stop to this but quite unable to do so. Instead, she pulled his sweater up over his head, shivering with pleasure as she enjoyed the sensation of his bare skin pressing down onto hers. Dani was vaguely aware of the phone ringing but ignored it, knowing nothing else was more important in this moment than the powerful physical desire she was feeling.

It was completely different from anything she'd experienced before.

Chapter Twenty Six

One of the techies had enhanced the video of Maisie Riddell. Bevan was showing it to her team on a screen she'd borrowed from another department. Her officers remained silent until the film had run its course.

'We're building up a whole new picture of this girl,' Dani began, stepping in front of Maisie's motionless image. 'Her mother had absolutely no idea about the life she was really living.'

Phil took over the narrative. 'Maisie had been performing in the Glasgow club scene since she'd turned fourteen years old. She sang in places that operated on the fringes of being legit. These were establishments where nobody asked too many questions.'

Andy put up his hand. 'How can Fiona not have known about this? Maisie must have been pulling some late nighters with this singing lark. Georgina couldn't *possibly* have been able to cover for her on *all* those occasions.'

'I don't think she did,' Phil said carefully. 'Remember that Georgie told me Maisie suspected her mum had a boyfriend? I think Fiona wasn't at home quite as much as she's been suggesting.'

Calder got to his feet. 'So what if Fiona found out all about this secret life? Maybe she confronted her daughter and they fought? Perhaps this sighting in Newcastle is a red-herring and Maisie never left Glasgow at all.'

Phil ran a hand through his silvery hair. 'I've known Fiona a long time. She couldn't have killed her daughter.'

'People do stuff in the heat of the moment, Phil,' Andy pressed his point, but not unkindly, 'that's why most murders are committed by someone known to the victim.'

Dani shook her head and frowned. 'But Fiona is very slight. Maisie was already taller and heavier than her mother. I can't see her killing the girl, even in a fit of rage.'

'What about this mysterious boyfriend, then?' Alice Mann put in. 'Might he have been involved in the confrontation? Fiona would certainly have needed help to get rid of the body.'

Phil took a step towards Dani, resting his hand on her arm. 'Could I speak with you for a moment, in private?'

Bevan looked at him closely, his expression struck her as odd. 'Right now?'

'Yes,' he replied flatly.

Dani instructed her team in their tasks and led the way to her office. When Phil was inside, she pulled the door shut, crossing her arms and eyeing her Sergeant expectantly.

'Do you recall there was a discrepancy in the timeline of Fiona's movements on the morning of Maisie's disappearance?'

Dani nodded patiently. 'She stopped for petrol and to buy a gift for her niece.'

'There's a coffee shop in that shopping centre. Fiona went there too.'

'How do you know this?' Dani furrowed her brow.

'Because she was meeting me.'

Bevan gestured for him to take a seat. She perched on the chair opposite, waiting for Phil to elaborate.

'Fiona and I have been sleeping together for about three months. It began after we took the girls to see a concert at the SECC.'

Bevan's mouth fell open and it took several seconds for any words to come out. 'Why the *hell* didn't you say anything sooner?'

'You know why.' The man sat quite impassively in front of her, his hands clasped together in his lap.

Dani felt a sudden urge to slap his face, but fought it back. 'Maisie has been missing for over a week and you're only telling me this *now*. You're one of the best policemen I've ever worked with – clever and decent and sensitive – all the qualities the force desperately needs in its officers.' She ran a hand through her hair. 'I don't think I can do anything to help you. Once this gets out, Phil, you're finished.'

He hung his head. 'I know it seems crazy, but I knew my relationship with Fiona had nothing to do with Maisie's disappearance, so I thought it was irrelevant to the investigation. We haven't seen one another since it all happened. I think it's over.'

'Did Maisie know about the two of you?'

Phil shook his head. 'From what Georgie said, Maisie must have suspected Fiona had a boyfriend. She didn't know it was me.'

Bevan wasn't convinced he could be so sure of that. 'I'm going to need the times and dates that the two of you were together.'

'Of course.' Phil lifted his gaze again. 'Fiona could never have harmed her daughter, that's why I had to tell you about our affair. I couldn't let the investigation proceed down a blind alley.'

'We have to discuss every possibility, every angle. Christ, Phil, you could be a *suspect* in this. If Maisie had found out about your relationship with her mother, it gives you a motive to get the girl out of the way – so she couldn't tell your family.'

'But she didn't know about us.' Phil looked panicky.

'You've obstructed my investigation, withheld vital information. This is an absolute bloody mess.'

'That seems like nothing compared to what I've done to Jane and the girls. I knew I shouldn't continue seeing her, but I was lonely and I wanted Fiona so badly. I don't suppose you'd understand.'

But she did. Dani understood only too well.

*

'What's going to happen to him?' Andy asked, the moment Dani approached his workstation.

'He's been suspended. We went to the DCS together. Phil told him everything.'

'Shit. I hope they take into account his years of service. This is the only slip-up the guy's ever made.'

'It's a bit more than a slip-up, Andy,' she said gently.

'For once, Phil Boag did something entirely for himself – not for his wife or his precious daughters. I sincerely hope he doesn't get crucified for it.'

Dani hadn't thought of it that way. 'Do you think there's any chance that Jane won't crucify him?'

Calder visibly shuddered. 'I wouldn't fancy having *that* conversation. Jane Boag makes the DCS seem like your fairy godmother.'

Bevan couldn't help but laugh, although her stomach was in knots for Phil. She really hoped he'd be okay. 'What implications does this have for the case, Andy? We've got to try and look at these new facts impartially.'

'Maisie might have found out about the affair. It could have been the trigger for her leaving home. Georgina was her best friend and her mother was playing an instrumental part in destroying her family.'

'Yes, it is possible. I'll have to re-brief the team.

But I don't think Fiona killed her daughter, Phil was right about that much. I believe her odd behaviour has been because of this relationship with Phil, not because she's lying about what happened to Maisie.'

'I agree. That guy Fiona went on a couple of dates with, Gavin Calhoun, he said that she suddenly ended contact with him. I bet that was when she started seeing Phil.'

Dani sighed. 'Did we miss the signs when we were working here with him? I truly thought that Phil was one of the good guys.'

'He is. Look, the girls are growing up now. Sorcha will be going off to university next year. Even Georgina must be spending more time out with her mates. Jane works all the hours God sends. What's Phil supposed to do, eh? He's just an ordinary, red-blooded male like the rest of us. Come on Dani, that set up was always too good to be true. He's had an affair, not put someone in hospital.'

Bevan snapped her head around. 'Why do you say that?'

'What?'

'About putting somebody in hospital?'

'I don't know. It was just a figure of speech, the first example that came into my head.'

She eyed him closely, but Andy simply appeared bemused and mildly pissed off. 'Right. Let's get focussed back on the case. We need to find out all the venues that Maisie performed in. That's where we'll unearth the people who provided her with a ticket out of Glasgow.'

Chapter Twenty Seven

Bill Hutchison was staring at the screen of the computer they kept on a desk in the study. A mug of tea was placed on one side of the keyboard and a pad and pen on the other. He was examining a marriage certificate, which he'd summoned up by using the online archives of the Scottish Records Office.

The details Bill was carefully transcribing were of the marriage between Terence Sinclair and Michelle Sinclair, née Peel, which took place at a Register Office in Aberdeen in 1996. Terry's ex-wife had been working as a hairdresser at the time of their wedding. He wondered if she did the same job now.

Hutchison knew he'd promised DCI Bevan and DS Boag that he would do no more digging, but when he spoke to DI Lyons on the phone, the man had left him with very little confidence that the case was being handled competently. If Erskine was on his trail, Bill felt he needed to keep one step ahead of him.

Armed with Michelle's maiden name, Bill was able to perform some Google searches in order to locate her current whereabouts. It didn't take long. Michelle was now the manageress of a beauty salon in Peebles. He was relieved, as this trip wouldn't be quite as onerous as the last one. Bill followed the link to their website and noted down the contact number and address, feeling really quite pleased with himself.

Thankfully, the salon was unisex and Bill was able to make an appointment for 3pm that afternoon. Half an hour beforehand, he walked up and down the street outside, gaining an idea of how the establishment operated. The people coming in and out were mostly of Joy's age group. Bill was fairly certain that this was a respectable sort of business. He entered the premises ten minutes early and sat reading a magazine on a bench by the window. Bill had asked to have his hair cut by Michelle herself, a request that wasn't treated as unusual, but meant he had to wait until she was finished with her previous client, a woman having a string of time-consuming treatments, all of which resulted in her looking faintly ridiculous, although Bill certainly didn't say so. He simply joined in with the chorus of 'oohs' and 'aahs' from the gaggle of ladies around him as she proudly sashayed out of the building.

Michelle was finally free to hustle him over to the sinks, instructing a young girl to give him a shampoo before depositing him back at one of the padded chairs, in front of a bank of mirrors.

'A short back and sides, please,' he asked genially, examining Michelle's reflection in the glass. She looked to be nearing fifty. Her voluminous hair was dyed a very dark brown and her skin artificially tanned, but her face was friendly and open.

Bill enquired about her business and what attractions there were to see in Peebles. Michelle chatted to him affably, this type of small-talk being a part of her job. Bill mentioned his grandsons and a recent weekend break he and Joy had enjoyed in Lochgilphead. Then the man took a deep breath, psyching himself up to ask his next question, only too aware that Michelle was wielding a pair of sharpened scissors. 'I hope you don't mind me asking, but were you once married to Terence Sinclair? I thought I recognised you from somewhere and I believe that must be it.'

Instead of doing him harm with them, the scissors abruptly slipped from Michelle's grasp, landing with a clatter onto the floor, where Bill's white hairs were scattered in clumps on the chequered tiles. 'Who sent you here?' She asked, through trembling lips.

'Nobody, I promise. I simply met the two of you once, in Aberdeen, many years ago.'

The woman seemed to suddenly snap out of her reverie. She bent down to retrieve the scissors, wiping them on her apron. 'Sorry about that. I've not heard Terry mentioned in a long time. We divorced a decade ago now.'

'Oh, that's a shame, I recalled you being happy together.'

'I don't think you can be recalling the right couple, Bill.' Michelle gave a sad smile. 'We weren't ever that.'

'Did you know that he died, up in Stonehaven a month or two back?'

She nodded. 'Aye, I saw it on the news. He looked years older than he should have done, in the photos they showed of him. His lifestyle finally caught up, I expect.'

'But he would have been out in the fresh air every day working at that boat yard. He probably had a healthier job than most folk.'

'That wasn't how he really made his money, Bill. When I found out how he earned his living, I got away from that man as soon as I humanly could. This was as far away from him as I could get without totally abandoning my old mum in Perth.'

Michelle had stopped cutting now and was holding a hand mirror up to the back of Bill's head, allowing him to survey her handiwork. He twisted around to look at her directly. 'What *did* Terry do for a living?'

Michelle glanced about her warily. 'Who are you? Why have you come here?'

'I want to know why someone killed Terence Sinclair.'

Michelle lowered her voice to a whisper. 'The real question, Bill, is why someone didn't do it years ago.'

*

When Bill drove back into Falkirk it was dark. He saw that the light was on in the kitchen window as he parked up at the house. Stepping into the hallway, he could smell the dinner cooking.

'I'm in here!' Joy called from the dining room.

Bill took off his coat and went to wash his hands. After that, he joined her. 'We don't often eat in here during the week,' he said in surprise.

'I thought we could sit and talk about what you discovered, dear.'

'I'm not sure you'll want to hear it, Joy.'

'You look tired, come and take a seat.' Joy poured her husband a brandy and brought in their plates of food. The aroma of the homemade stew seemed to revive him.

'She was a nice lady, Michelle Peel. After my haircut she led me into the back for a coffee, there's a flat behind the shop that she lives in. It's perfectly pleasant.'

'Did she tell you about Sinclair?'

Bill nodded, taking a sip of the brandy to restore his spirits. 'When they were first married, they had a house in Aberdeen. Terence had a reasonably respectable job at the harbour. He worked for one of the shipping companies. Then, out of the blue, Sinclair was arrested. He was accused of trying to smuggle items coming over from Europe on the container ships, stuff that wasn't being declared through customs. There wasn't enough evidence to convict him but he lost his job. Michelle was upset about it, but they didn't split up then, that came later. Sinclair got other jobs, on the building sites and on the boats. He scraped together a living for them both. But Terence was spending more and more nights away from home. Michelle thought he had another woman, so she followed him one evening. Sinclair went to the Fisherman's Bar. His wife couldn't follow him inside - she would have been far too conspicuous. She sat outside in her car for an hour instead. Then Michelle decided to have a look around. She went down a grimy alleyway to the back of the pub. The door was propped open, because a man was cooking in the kitchens and it was full of steam.

Next to the kitchen, was a carpeted staircase leading up to the first floor. She doesn't quite know why, but Michelle walked up those stairs. From halfway, she could hear voices, chattering and laughing. Michelle pressed herself into the grubby wall, tip-toeing the rest of the way, until she'd nearly reached the top. She stopped and listened. There was a man's voice, it was her husband. He was negotiating with another man. They were sharing a joke. It was the most horrible joke Michelle had ever heard.

When the men seemed to have moved away, she poked her head around the top of the stairs. There was a long hallway, with doors lining both sides. The same reddish, dirty carpet ran the length of it. Terry was nowhere to be seen. Then, one of the doors opened. A girl stepped out of it, dressed in a short nightgown and not much else. Michelle watched her in that doorway for several minutes, quite unable to believe her eyes. Michelle said the girl was young, so young that she felt the stinging bile rise up into her throat.

She turned and ran, back down the staircase and out into the night. Michelle gulped in the air like she'd stumbled upon a watering hole in the middle of a desert. She got into the car and drove home; packing a bag and going straight back to her mum's place.'

Joy sat perfectly still, with the meal untouched before her. 'Did Michelle go to the police?'

'No, she just left Terence, filed for divorce and never set eyes upon him again.'

'DCI Bevan must raid that terrible place and get those girls out of there.'

Bill looked at her plaintively. 'But I promised the police I wasn't going to do any more meddling, Joy. They won't want to hear what I've found out.'

His wife leant across the table and took his hand. 'This is Danielle we're talking about. *Of course*, she'll want to hear it. DCI Bevan could never ignore a crime she'd been notified about. It wouldn't matter how long ago it happened, she would always take action. I'm sure of it, Bill.'

He nodded with relief. 'You're right, yes. I don't know how I could ever have doubted it. I'll call her first thing in the morning.'

Chapter Twenty Eight

In the cold light of day, Bill's reservations had returned. Something was making him hesitate to contact DCI Bevan. She'd told him repeatedly to stop sticking his nose into police business. The Riddell girl was still missing and he didn't like to bother her.

But Michelle's sickening story was imprinted in his mind's eye. At breakfast time, all he could visualise was that long red corridor, with doors leading off either side. Then he remembered the girl he saw in the kitchens of the Fisherman's Bar. The thought of her being shut up behind one of those doors was almost more than he could bear.

Bill rushed into the study and located his address book. He flicked impatiently through the pages. Bill knew that Andy Calder thought he was a crackpot. DS Boag had been more patient with him, but he sensed the man didn't hold him in much higher regard. Bill paused for a moment when he found the entry he was looking for. He briefly prevaricated over the extravagance of making an international call at this hour of the morning, but quickly dismissed his concerns, remembering that the fate of those poor girls was a stake. Bill went out into the hall, lifted the receiver and placed the call.

'Hello,' said a distant, sleepy voice.

'Oh, I hope I've not woken you up Detective Sharpe. It's Bill here, Bill Hutchison.'

'Is everything okay, Bill? Is Dani alright?'

'Yes, as far as I am aware, she's absolutely fine.'

'Then what can I do for you?' His tone was puzzled but not unfriendly.

'I've got a problem, Detective Sharpe. You were the only person I could think of who might be able to help me.'

*

Dieter had stocked Dani's cupboards with food. He was busily preparing proper pancakes, with fresh blueberries and maple syrup. The DCI carried across a large pot of coffee, clearing a space on the table and setting it down. She padded back to the kitchen area and rested her head on Dieter's shoulder.

'When have you got to go home?'

'In a couple of days. You could always take some leave and come back to Norway with me? You've hardly seen the best parts of my country yet.' Dieter turned round and placed a tender kiss on her lips.

'I can't do that in the middle of a case. I'm a man down as it is, with Phil suspended from duty.'

'It seems crazy to have such a good policeman stuck at home, twiddling his thumbs.'

'Well, he *has* stepped over the line. Withholding evidence in a murder investigation is incredibly serious.'

Dieter said nothing, carrying the frying pan to the table and sliding a couple of pancakes onto a plate. 'Are you still checking out the clubs where Maisie worked as a singer?'

'Yes, Andy and I are liaising with Vice to come up with a list of the most likely venues. The problem is the people who run these places are impossible to find in the daytime. The clubs are boarded up and the owners simply disappear off the face of the earth.'

'They are nocturnal animals,' Dieter said with a grin. 'The sunlight doesn't agree with them.'

Dani leant forward and touched her hand to his face. 'I will miss you.'

He locked his fingers through hers and brushed his lips against her palm. 'I'll come back again - if you want me to.'

She smiled. 'You know I want that very much.'

*

Sam Sharpe sat in the passenger seat of Bill's car. He unzipped his padded jacket and gratefully received the take-out cup of coffee handed to him. 'I've got no more authority to be doing this than you have,' he stated wryly.

'Yes, but you have got the training and the expertise,' Bill replied.

The American gave a thin smile. 'I'm flattered you've got so much faith in me.'

'I do appreciate you coming all this way to help.'

'If there's a chance of nailing Erskine, I'm not gonna pass it up. I'm here on my own time, but if my boss knew about it, he'd be behind me a hundred percent. The fact that Richard Erskine got off after killing a US citizen still rankles in my department.'

It was getting dark. They were watching the exterior of the Fisherman's Bar, at the dockside in Aberdeen. Several men had already entered the premises, but it was still early.

'I believe that Erskine discovered Terence Sinclair was in the business of exploiting young girls. That's why he killed him. Erskine was meting out some kind of primitive justice against a man that mistreated vulnerable women,' Bill said quietly. 'Just as his grandmother had herself been abused.'

Sam shifted round to look at his friend. 'Don't make the mistake of glorifying what Richard Erskine's done. Mackie Shaw hadn't harmed anyone, yet he was murdered in the same, horrible way. Erskine's developed a taste for it. He enjoys the killing, but now he's manufactured some kind of justification for what he does. That's all, pure and simple. I'm not saying Terence Sinclair was a great guy, but he should have been put on trial for his crimes and his operation shut down. With Erskine's method, these shitbags are quickly replaced by someone else – nothing changes.'

'I see your point, Detective Sharpe.'

'Now, when did your hairdresser lady say that she saw the girls working the top floor of this joint?'

'It was back in the winter of 2009, the January or February she thinks.'

'That's a long time ago, Bill.'

'I know. But I saw that young woman here last week. The landlady called her Anita. I don't believe for a second that was her real name.'

'Right. Here's what we're gonna do. You're gonna go in there and order a drink. Chat to this landlady for a while. Drop a few hints that you might be interested in a little female company this evening. She already suspects that you may be up for it. Don't say anything directly, let her do the talking. I'll be waiting round the back. If she leads you upstairs, make sure you assess what's going on up there and then say you've left your cash out in the car or something, and you'll be back in a minute – just get the hell out of there. Once we've got our proof, we can take it to the local cops. Let them do a raid.'

Bill's face was ashen. 'I'm not sure I can manage that.'

'Sure you can.' Sam slapped him on the back. 'I'll be just outside if you think you're in any danger.'

The older man nodded his head and swung his legs out of the car. As he walked towards the entrance, Bill felt his resolve wavering. Then he thought about that bewildered young girl working in the kitchens, and he stood up straighter, pushing his way through the heavy door.

Liz recognised him. As he approached the bar she'd already poured him out a beer. 'Sorry, I've forgotten your name. But you came in asking about Terry?'

'That's right. It's Bill.'

The bar was gradually filling up. A game of pool was in full swing in a dark alcove in the corner. Several clusters of men sat at the small tables dotted about the room, staring at the muted television set attached to a wall. It suddenly struck him as surreal to imagine there was a brothel operating just upstairs. He nearly downed his pint and bolted for the car park. But something made him stand his ground. If they were wrong, the worst that could happen would be his short-term humiliation. But if they were right, he couldn't leave those girls in that awful situation.

Bill turned back towards Liz, playing with the pint glass in his hand. 'Terry talked to me about this place a lot.'

'Oh yes, all good I hope.'

'He said you catered for all kinds of tastes here.'

Liz stopped arranging the bottles on the back of the bar and turned to face him. She leant her arms on the counter, her sparkly top clattering against the wood. 'And what are your particular tastes, Bill?'

'That girl I saw the other night, Anita. Is she still here?'

Liz pursed her lips. 'Anita had to go home. But there are others like her. You can't be too choosy Bill.'

He nodded. 'Of course. Maybe you could make a selection for me? I think you'd be good at that.'

Liz glanced over his shoulder, eyeing her clientele closely. She lowered her voice. 'We've had some new faces in recently, hanging around and asking questions. Finish your drink and leave out the front.

I'll meet you by the back door in five minutes.'

Bill dipped his head in acknowledgment. Liz hurried off to serve another customer. He supped up and lifted his coat. As he slipped off the stool it almost felt as if his legs had turned to jelly. It took the most monumental effort for him to reach the door without them buckling. Once Bill was out in the fresh air, he gained a little strength. Glancing over to the car, he saw that Sam wasn't in the front seat. He ducked around the side of the building. The alleyway was just as Michelle had described it. Bill reached the back door and waited.

'Sam! Are you there?' He whispered into the shadows.

'I'm here,' he rasped in reply, not showing himself. 'As soon as you've seen what you need to, get the hell out of there, okay.'

At that moment, the door was wrenched open. Liz peered through a tiny gap and gestured for him to enter. The red carpet was gone, replaced by an equally cheap looking linoleum.

'Straight up the stairs,' she said matter-of-factly. 'Stevie will sort you out.'

Bill solemnly climbed the steps, like a condemned man ascending the gallows. What was disconcerting him was the eerie quietness. He wasn't quite sure what kinds of noises he expected to hear. At the top of the flight he turned right.

There was the corridor.

At the end of it sat a weasel-like little man at a desk. The corridor seemed to go on for ever, Bill's legs felt like lead weights as he dragged himself along it.

He finally reached the man. 'Liz sent me up,' he explained weakly.

'Door two,' the weasel replied, not even glancing up from the tabloid he was reading.

'Shall I pay now, or after?'

'After.'

Bill noticed then that the doors were all numbered. The second door was back down the corridor again. He stopped in front of it, feeling as if his heart might explode out of his chest. Bill knocked gently, twisting the handle at the same time. He stepped inside and closed the door behind him. The girl was sitting on the edge of an unmade bed. Some effort had been made to make the room comfortable. Chintzy curtains hung at the window and there was a nice wardrobe and bedside table.

'Do you speak English?' He whispered.

'Yes,' she replied.

Bill went straight to the wardrobe and found it was actually full of clothes. He picked out a top and some trousers and handed them to her. He was gripped with a strange determination. Bill knew it wasn't part of the plan but he really didn't care.

'Would you mind putting them on?' He said decisively. 'I'm going to get you out of here.'

Chapter Twenty Nine

'Holy crap, Bill. You've sure got a problem with using official channels.' Sam turned up the heating as they raced out of the car park of the Fisherman's Bar. A young girl sat shivering in the back seat, wrapped in the detective's padded jacket.

'I couldn't just leave her there.'

Sam twisted round. 'What's your name, sweetheart?'

'Freya,' she muttered, through chattering teeth.

'We're gonna take you to the police station, is that okay? They'll find a decent hostel for you to spend the night in.'

'I would like to go home. Coming here was not as they said it would be.'

'Where is home, Freya?' He asked gently.

'Lithuania.'

'How many other girls were with you in that place?'

'There were six of us. Will you get the others out too?'

'I hope so,' Sam replied. He shifted back to face the front. 'Although, they might be long gone by now.'

'I realise I acted rashly, Detective Sharpe. But the man guarding them was engrossed in his newspaper. I was able lead Freya out of the room and down the stairs before anyone noticed. Even if I had bolted on my own, they would still have known something was up.'

'Let's head straight to the station. This DI Lyons might still be able to get some incriminating evidence from the scene.'

Bill grunted. 'I'm not sure that DI Lyons would know what to look for.'

'Hey, not all of us detectives are incompetent,' Sam gave a chuckle.

'Speaking of which, I should really give DCI Bevan a call and tell her what's happened.'

'Well, if you do, please don't mention that I'm here.'

Bill shot him a puzzled look. 'Danielle would love to see you, I'm sure.'

'That's as maybe, but we have an arrangement. It doesn't include dropping in on one another unannounced – particularly when there's a big case going down. I don't want to put Dani under any pressure. That's not how our relationship works.'

Bill nodded, not really understanding this modern sounding situation. 'If that's what you want, I won't say a word to her.'

'Great. That's what I want.'

*

DCs Calder and Mann travelled together in the lift to the Serious Crime Division.

'It's like we've hit a brick wall,' Andy lamented.

'Well, very few people are going to admit to employing an underage girl. The club owners don't want us to know they've had fourteen year olds on the premises.'

'But you'd think one of the guys who Maisie performed with might actually give a crap what's happened to her.'

Andy strode towards DCI Bevan's office, ready to give her the lowdown on their trip to the west-end. Dani waved him in. She had a perturbed look on her face. Before Calder could say anything, his boss explained, 'I've just had a call from Aberdeen. Bill Hutchison has uncovered a child prostitution racket operating out of the docks there.'

Andy took a seat, even though he'd not been invited to. 'Good old Bill, I didn't know he had it in him.'

'When Bill thinks he's onto something, he's like a dog with a bone,' Dani muttered darkly. 'The man could have got himself killed. Apparently, he smuggled a young Lithuanian girl out of the place single-handed. Bill took her straight to the police station and reported the gang. DI Lyons authorised a raid and they've managed to round up all the girls. They'd been bundled into a van, ready to transport to some other anonymous hell hole.'

'Will they be making arrests?'

'Only a couple, the others had scarpered. But if Lyons can get one of them to talk, they could bust the whole operation.'

'I'm not even going to ask how Hutchison pulled that one off on his own. He's certainly done better than me and Alice. Nobody's saying anything about Maisie working the club scene.'

'Not many folk are going to invite a storm to come down on their heads.' Dani walked back over to her desk.

Andy remained seated. The words that Dani had just spoken were circling around in his head. 'Do you recall Alex Ritchie?'

'Maisie's next door neighbour, the boy with learning difficulties?'

'They used to play music together, before Maisie was doing it for real. Only Alex mentioned they had this favourite band, called the Storm. They must be some indie group, because I've never heard of them.'

'Do you want to check it out? It's a long shot, but you never know.'

Andy nodded, he stood up, ready to return to his desk.

'Hold the fort for me will you?' Dani asked, 'I'm going to pay Phil a visit and see how he's doing. I want to be sure to catch him alone.'

'Of course, Ma'am.'

It took about half an hour for Bevan to drive to the Boags' house in Pollockshaws. When Phil answered the door he looked tired.

'Hello Ma'am, come in.' He led her across an impressive hallway into a spanking new kitchen. The marble worktops were dazzlingly white and seemed to have sparkling stones worked into them. Dani did her best not to gawp, as Phil put the kettle on.

'How are you?' She asked tentatively.

'I haven't slept much. I told Jane about me and Fiona last night. We've not said anything to the girls yet.' He perched on a stool next to her.

'I'm really sorry.' Dani placed her hand on his arm. She found herself strangely curious to know how Jane reacted to the news. 'Do the girls need to find out?'

Phil shrugged. 'We aren't at the stage of deciding stuff like that. I don't think Jane has absorbed the information properly. When I was telling her, it actually seemed like she didn't believe me.'

'It is quite out of character,' Dani commented. 'But the fact your wife didn't see it coming shows how much she was taking you for granted.'

'Do you think?' Phil got up to make the coffees. 'Now everyone at work has found out, it's like I've woken from a dream. I can't imagine why I ever did something so reckless and stupid.'

'But Fiona seems like a nice woman. She was on her own and so were you. I can see exactly why you did it.'

Phil brought the mugs over and sat by Dani

again. 'I'm not on my own though, am I? I've got Jane and the girls. We have a system, it isn't always perfect, but we make it work for us as a family.'

Dani sighed, taking his hand. 'It obviously wasn't working for you, Phil.'

'Does that matter? When you're responsible for the happiness of others you've got to forget your own needs.'

Dani thought about what Andy Calder had said. 'Your girls are growing up. You can't forfeit your happiness for their benefit forever. If you still love Jane, fair enough, try and make it work. But she's got to meet you half way.'

Phil nodded, his eyes glassy with tears. 'Isn't it weird how things appear so clear from the outside. When you're wrapped up in the situation yourself, it's really hard to know where you're going wrong.'

'You'll find a way. I know you will.'

'However this whole thing turns out,' Phil added with determination, 'I certainly won't be telling any more lies.'

Chapter Thirty

'The Storm' turned out to be a group of music students from Strathclyde University. They'd released a couple of albums which had sold pretty well online. Andy was meeting their lead guitarist after his lectures finished for lunch.

Calder hung around the cafeteria waiting for the lad to turn up. Having never been a student, he found these places disconcerting. Very few of the kids he knew growing up had gone to university. When he joined the police at sixteen, his contemporaries thought he'd moved into a new social class, leaving his friends and family behind. Most of his pals now were fellow officers on the force, or couples he'd met through Carol.

Callum Forbes picked Calder out easily. He was the oldest and smartest dressed person in the place. Forbes' hair was gelled up in a spike above his head and he wore the most incredibly tight jeans the detective had ever seen. It made the lad's legs look like a pair of sticks. Andy couldn't understand why he would want to appear in public that way.

'DC Calder, how may I help you?' Forbes put out a hand.

From his polished manners, Andy immediately wondered if he was a public school type. 'I'm investigating the disappearance of Maisie Riddell.'

Callum looked puzzled. 'I don't think I can assist you with that.'

'You've heard about the case then?'

'Yeah, I've seen it on the news. It's really sad.'

'Did you know that Maisie was a big fan of your

band?'

'No, I didn't. But the Storm's got a lot of fans online. My Twitter account has over 300,000 followers.'

Andy felt his heart sink. 'Okay, well thanks for your time.' Calder rummaged in his pocket for the photograph, just in case it jogged a memory. 'This is Maisie. She was fourteen years old and had a great singing voice. Apparently, she'd performed a few gigs around the city, but we've not been able to find out where.'

Callum looked at the image closely. 'I'd not seen a picture of her before. She's kind of familiar.'

Andy waited patiently, trying not to get his hopes up.

'She's called Maisie, did you say?'

The detective nodded.

'It's just that we used to get these letters, about a year ago, from a girl who liked our stuff. I wouldn't normally remember, but it's actually really unusual to receive something handwritten these days. And we weren't that big back then, either. What she wrote was kind of personal, too. So it stuck in my mind. I've still got them. One time, she attached a photo. I think this might have been her, but she signed off using a different name.'

'Can I see them, just to check?'

'Sure. Let me grab a sandwich and I'll take you up to my room.'

*

Andy returned to Pitt Street with the letters inside a plastic evidence bag. He'd wanted to examine them more closely back at the station. Forbes was right. The girl had enclosed a photograph with her first letter. It was taken on holiday, clearly a while back, but Andy was fairly sure it was Maisie.

Calder spread out the correspondence carefully

on his desk. Pulling on a pair of latex gloves, he began to read through them all, in date order. After scanning a couple of sheets, he searched in his drawer for a pad. Unusually for him, he began to take notes of what he was reading. In these letters, Maisie was referring to herself as Kenna Adams, but the details she was giving of her life very closely matched those of the missing girl.

Kenna was describing how her parents had split up when she was nine years old, before her father moved abroad. Calder could sense from the raw emotions she poured onto these pages that the girl had been harbouring a great deal of resentment about the divorce. The letters were clearly her way of sharing these thoughts and feelings with someone else, even if the recipient never replied. Kenna discussed the way she'd become disconnected from her mother, who spent a lot of time at work and refused to speak with her daughter about her dad.

A gush of anguish spilled out into the documents when Kenna described her father's announcement that he was planning to marry again. His fiancé was young and from the place her dad now lived. It meant he would probably start a new family and never come back to Scotland. Worse than this, Kenna did not take to her father's new wife. The girl would spend her Christmases with them and she found the woman prickly and unkind.

Andy wasn't sure whether these particular letters were based on fact or fiction. He wondered if Maisie was using the character of Kenna to create a fantasy world based around her own life. Calder wanted to discuss this with Dani, to discover her take on it. She would be more able to interpret the nuances of the text than he was.

It was getting late, but Andy was sure his DCI would still be up. She'd dropped in to see Phil earlier in the day and had surely gone straight home to her flat afterwards. He carefully placed the bundle of letters back in its plastic wrapping and left the building.

Calder went via Scotstounhill on his way home. He parked up at the kerb and lifted the package from the passenger seat. Dani's hallway was in darkness. Andy wondered if she might already be in bed and was about to turn away when he spotted a silhouette at the end of the corridor. He put his face up to the glass and peered more closely. The kitchen at the back of the property was only dimly lit, but the figures of Dieter Karlsen and his boss were clearly outlined against the fading light spilling through the patio door. Their bodies were entwined, lips firmly joined and hands tugging desperately at the other's clothes, as if locked in some strange, tribal dance.

Andy whipped his head back, the sight causing him to physically recoil. He strode quickly to where the car was parked, tossed the letters inside and threw himself into the driving seat. Not quite knowing why he was so angry, the detective stabbed the key into the ignition and sped away.

Chapter Thirty One

Calder sent a text to his boss first thing in the morning. It said he'd be in a bit later than usual. He was going to follow up on a lead he'd got from his interview with the band member from the Storm. This wasn't a lie, exactly. Andy had decided to show Carol the letters. It was unorthodox, but he needed someone else's opinion. For the first time in their professional relationship, he didn't want it to be Dani's.

Andy made a pot of coffee for his wife, withdrawing to squat on the rug in the lounge, playing with Amy whilst she read them through. An hour later, he returned to the kitchen, with the toddler perched happily on his hip. Carol had removed her glasses and was looking thoughtful.

'What did you make of Maisie's step-mother when you were in Norway?' She asked.

'We only met Kristin Riddell the one time. I must admit I didn't warm to her, but she seemed devoted to the little boy.'

'If this Kenna character does represent Maisie, then she really disliked her step-mother.'

'But do you think the things she writes about her are true?'

Carol sighed. 'It's difficult to say. Girls of that age do have their fantasies. Kristin symbolised everything that had gone wrong in her life. You couldn't blame Maisie for hating her. At the same time, she makes some fairly specific accusations in these letters. Can you investigate them to see if they're true?'

'I'd have to work with the detectives in Stavanger again. I'm not sure that's such a good idea,' Andy said, making a face.

'Isn't Detective Karlsen already here, staying at Dani's place. Why don't you run it by him?'

Andy grunted. 'The guy's on leave. He won't be able to do any more than me.'

'What about the other one, the lady. You said she was a better detective anyway.'

He laid a hand on his wife's back, allowing Amy to slide into her mother's arms. 'Actually, that's a good idea. I don't really trust Karlsen. It's probably best he's not there.' Andy leant down and gave them both a kiss. 'Thanks Carol, you've been a great help.'

*

Back at his workstation, Andy checked that Dani wasn't around. According to the replacement DS, she was in a meeting with Nicholson, a man he harboured a barely disguised hatred for. Striding over with confidence, he shouldered the flimsy door and entered Dani's office. Her desk diary was lying open and a thick address book sat next to it. Andy lifted the leather-bound tome casually and flicked through to the numbers he needed. Not wishing to push his luck, he took a snapshot of the page on his phone and returned to his own desk.

Magda Hustad answered after a couple of rings, she sounded stressed.

'Detective Hustad? It's Andy Calder here, from Strathclyde Police.'

'Oh, hello Andy, how can I help, has there been a development?'

'That's what I'm trying to find out. It seems Maisie may have made some allegations against her step-mother. I've outlined the key facts in an e-mail. It should be in your inbox now. I wondered if you could do a few checks on Kristin Riddell for me?'

'Sure, not a problem.' The woman sighed. 'I'll get on to it as quickly as I can, but we're very busy here.'

'I understand, Magda.'

There was a brief pause before she continued, 'I know this may sound odd, but have you seen Detective Karlsen at all?'

'Why do you ask?' Andy tried to keep his tone neutral.

'He is currently on leave and I can't get hold of him on his mobile. I desperately need to pass on a message.'

'I could ask DCI Bevan, she may have heard from him,' he replied carefully. 'What's the message?'

'The Chief of Police has sent a man in to audit our unsolved cases. He is shaking everything up here at the Bureau. If you tell Dieter that, he will know to call me.'

'Okay, if we have any contact with Karlsen, I'll pass that on.'

'Look, I've got to go.'

'No bother, thanks for your help.' Andy replaced the phone. Now he was really intrigued. Why was Magda so flustered about having their previous cases re-examined? He wondered if she and Dieter always played things by the book. Magda had seemed pretty straight to him. Karlsen he wasn't so sure about. Andy looked up as Dani strode past him, returning to her office. She took off her jacket and beckoned him over. Andy felt uncomfortable as he entered the room. He wasn't used to keeping things from his boss.

'When I was in with the DCS, I received a call. There's been a murder down on London Road. The squad who were called to the scene think the dead man is Clive Anton. The SIO thought we might be interested.'

'Let's get over there straight away, Ma'am.'

*

The street outside Anton's boarded up nightclub had been sealed off with tape. A couple of uniforms were guarding the door which led up to Anton's flat.

Dani flashed her ID. 'Is the body up there?' She enquired.

The PC shook his head. 'It's actually in a shed out the back, but you can only reach it through the flat.'

The wind was whistling through Clive Anton's apartment. Much to Dani's relief, this had blown away the sickly sweet smell that had permeated the place when she was last here. The techies had set down trays along the corridor leading to the kitchen. The back door was wide open and revealed a set of exterior steps which took them down into the back yard. This was where all the action was going on.

Dani introduced herself and Andy to the SIO, DI Jilly Reid. 'What have we got?' She asked.

'His throat's been cut. Quite a professional job, I'd say. Anton used this old shed as a kind of workshop. He re-upholstered furniture, if you can believe it. His stuff is actually rather good.'

'Can I have a look?' Dani asked warily.

'Of course.' Jilly stood back and allowed her colleagues to enter.

Dani and Andy glanced at each other, not needing to put into words what they were both thinking. Clive Anton had been placed on one of his own, throne-like chairs. His neck was a bloody gash. Behind him, blood was sprayed up the walls like a piece of modern art. Anton's hands lay in his lap, palms facing upwards.

Andy glanced at his boss. 'Bloody hell,' he muttered darkly.

Chapter Thirty Two

It was only lunchtime, but Bevan and Calder stopped for a drink in one of the pubs further along London Road.

'Is that what the crime scene looked like in this case Bill Hutchison has been harping on about – the one up in Stonehaven?' Andy asked, taking a long sip of beer.

'I only saw the photos, but it was very similar, yes.' Dani had allowed herself a small white wine.

'It's just like the murder of Mackie Shaw. There's certainly no denying it.'

'The details of the murder on Garansay were reported in the press after the trial of Richard Erskine, weren't they? This could be someone trying to replicate the same conditions.'

'It could be, but then why was Erskine watching Bill and Joy's house? Much as I think the old guy's a bit flaky, he might actually be onto something.'

Dani spent a few moments admiring the Victorian fittings around the bar, her mind running through all the things Bill had been trying to tell her for the past few weeks. She turned to address Andy directly. 'Terence Sinclair was part of a prostitution racket, right? They were exploiting underage girls from Eastern Europe. What if Richard Erskine found out about this gang and decided to execute Sinclair? Perhaps he sees himself as the protector of these vulnerable women, because of what his grandmother had gone through?'

'So how does Clive Anton fit into it?'

'When we were at Anton's flat before, there was

this smell of perfume everywhere. It was so overpowering it made me want to be sick. Phil said that his daughter Sorcha wears the same brand. Apparently, it's what all her friends are using.'

'So Anton had young girls there, at his flat.'

'The place is above the club, just like Sinclair's operation was based in the floor above the Fisherman's Bar. Maybe Erskine's been watching these places and working out what they're up to.'

'Erskine's clever. He never leaves forensic traces.' Andy polished off his half pint.

'The SIOs in these cases haven't even got Erskine in the frame. At the moment, he's free to come and go as he chooses. We've got no idea who he's earmarked as his next victim.'

'But these scumbags he's bumping off – can we really describe them as *victims*?'

'Oh yes. Erskine's made them into victims. These people needed to be tried in a court of law and their guilt proven. How does Erskine really know he's targeting the right people? He might make a mistake and kill an innocent man.'

'He hasn't done that so far, Ma'am. I suppose Erskine thinks we haven't managed all that well at tracking these bastards down ourselves. Let's face it, he wouldn't be far wrong.'

Dani took another sip of wine. There wasn't much she could say to argue with that. It was perfectly true.

*

Joy had prepared a special meal, laying the table formally for their guest. Bill and Sam were enjoying a pre-dinner drink in the lounge. When the food was ready, Joy called the men in to eat.

'This is really lovely, Mrs Hutchison. I can't recall

the last time I ate a home cooked meal, probably when I visited my mom for Thanksgiving.'

'I just hope you enjoy what I've made.' Joy gestured for them to take a seat and hurried into the kitchen to gather the plates. When she returned, Bill paused to say Grace, before his wife leant over the table and dished up. 'I think you've both been so brave. If you hadn't got those girls out of that terrible place I swear I'd never have felt at peace ever again.'

'Well, it was the police that raided the joint,' Sam explained.

'Come on,' Joy added sternly, 'if it hadn't been for the two of you highlighting what was going on there, those people would still be in operation. Any news on Freya?'

'She's still at the hostel. DI Lyons told me she will receive counselling before they consider sending her back to Lithuania,' said Bill.

'I should think so too, after what the poor girl's been through. It's awful to imagine such things going on in this country. I hope you informed the detective that Freya is welcome to stay here with us. We have plenty of room. I would take good care of her.'

'Yes, I did. But the idea was too unorthodox for the Detective Inspector to contemplate.'

Joy tutted disapprovingly.

'To be fair to the guy, it isn't how these situations work. The authorities would have to vet you for weeks beforehand, if they were to let the girl become your responsibility. It's enough that you got her out of that place, Bill.'

'But it upsets me to picture all the other, similar establishments that still exist out there.' Bill sipped his wine and looked wistful.

Sam put down his knife and fork. 'You can't afford to think that way. As a cop, I see terrible stuff on a daily basis and you try your best not to brood on it. We work hard and do what we can to help. It's not possible to save everyone who is in difficult circumstances.'

Bill nodded. 'Yes, but it's hard not to feel for them, just the same.'

Sam carried on eating, he wasn't sure it was possible to stop Bill Hutchison from carrying the burdens of the world on his shoulders. It was probably a better idea to distract him instead. 'Did you speak with Dani in the end?'

'DI Lyons said he would call her. I haven't had the opportunity yet.' Bill caught the American's eye. 'You know, I've been worried about the DCI recently, she hasn't been herself. I really think you should contact her. I sense she needs guidance.'

'I've left plenty of messages.' Sam sighed. 'She's not got back to me.'

'But Dani still doesn't know that you're in the country?'

Sam shook his head.

'I don't understand why the two of you aren't together right now. When you love someone, that's where you need to be, isn't it?'

Chapter Thirty Three

Magda Hustad was snowed under with paperwork. She'd still not heard from Dieter and was finding it increasingly tricky to steer his replacement away from the Aron Holm case. Magda knew they'd only taken very cursory statements from Holm's work colleagues who were at the restaurant that night. It was going to be obvious to this Inspector as soon as he read them.

When the Scottish detectives came and started digging around into the assault on Holm, Magda hadn't found it so bad. She knew they just wanted to find the lost girl. Magda had liked the pair and didn't sense either of them was vindictive. Knowing there wasn't much more she could do at the Bureau, Hustad decided to chase up Andy Calder's lead instead. After all, she also wanted young Maisie Riddell returned safely to her mother.

Her first recourse was to visit Andreas Nilsen, at his parents' house on the hill. It was a glorious day and Magda paused to take in the view of the morning sun, shimmering on the lake. Nilsen appeared to be home alone. He led her into the living room, which possessed a bank of windows facing the water.

'Why would anyone wish to destroy this beautiful country?' He asked sadly, as he observed her eyes being drawn to the vista outside.

'Is that what you believe the oil companies are doing?'

'Of course. It is all about profit. They make money now and the future generations suffer.'

'But we need energy. Look at this lovely house your parents have. You don't want to go back to the dark ages.' Magda directed her gaze at his earnest young face.

The man smiled. 'There are alternatives, Detective. But our corporations and governments are too short-sighted to investigate them. Only Aron Holm is putting forward a new strategy. We have to hope that the future is led by men such as him. Now, I don't believe you have come to talk to me about my views on the environment.'

'How well do you know Kristin Riddell?'

Andreas seemed taken aback. 'She was Charles Riddell's secretary at Barents Oil, then she married him. That's all.'

'I have been looking into her past.'

'Oh yes?'

'Kristin Berg attended the same university as you.'

'She must have been a few years above me. I don't recall her.'

'But Kristin is very beautiful. I'm surprised you don't remember seeing her there.'

Andreas said nothing.

'She studied Environmental Sciences and graduated with honours. It was something of a come down for her to become a secretary, don't you think?'

The man rested his weight on the arm of the sofa, his eyes fixed on the distant horizon. 'Kristin fell in love with him, pure and simple.'

'But she was a member of your organisation?'

'At first, yes, she was. It was my master plan - to get one of our members on the inside of a big corporation like Barents Oil. Kristin's family are well-regarded business people in Stavanger. It was easy for her to get the job.'

'Did she provide you with much information?'

'In the first year, it was fantastic. We had the inside track on every new proposal, every potential exploration site. We could target our message accordingly. Then Kristin began to become more cautious, more reticent. It would take several days for her to return my calls. She would say that it was important to leak the details slowly, otherwise her bosses would become suspicious. Little did I realise that Kristin was being absorbed into their world, being brainwashed by their self-justifying arguments.'

'When did she tell you about her relationship with Charles?'

'A week before the wedding.' Andreas turned to Magda. 'It came as something of a surprise, as you can imagine, although she'd been cold with me for months, hardly wanting me to touch her anymore. I thought the strain of leading a double life was tiring her out.'

'Does Charles know she used to be in your organisation, that she was your lover?'

'You will think me sentimental Detective Hustad, but I simply let her go. I loved Kristin, so I said nothing at all.'

'Do you know that Charles Riddell's daughter found out about Kristin's past?'

Andreas looked surprised. 'I didn't even know he had a daughter until the detectives from Glasgow came and questioned me. It actually wouldn't be that difficult to find out, with access to the internet and online records being what they are. I'm sure if you visited our website, you might easily find a photograph with Kristin in it – as part of a demonstration perhaps. I always wondered if Charles knew the truth really, he just chose not to acknowledge it.'

'Weren't you angry with Kristin – didn't you want

revenge?'

'What, enough to snatch her baby for half an hour or kidnap a teenager? If I wanted to get even with Kristin I would simply tell Charles the truth, show him the photographs of us together, when we were happy. Force him to face what in his heart he already knows.'

Magda nodded. 'Thank you for your time, Andreas.'

They walked to the front door together.

'Detective Karlsen is not with you today?'

'He's on leave,' Magda replied.

'You need to cut yourself free of that one. He's no good.'

Magda said nothing, stepping out into the bright sunshine and making her way slowly back to the car, allowing the powerful rays to gently warm her back.

Chapter Thirty Four

It was the first time that year Dani had stood out in her little garden and enjoyed the sunshine. Dieter stepped through the patio door to join her, slipping his arm around her narrow waist.

'I've booked my flight for tomorrow morning,' he spoke quietly into her ear.

Dani felt the words make her stomach turn over. She dreaded the moment they would have to say goodbye. 'It's all sorted then.'

'I've got to go. I can't leave Magda with all that work to do.'

'No, of course not. You must return.' Dani moved out of his embrace and went into the house. She placed her empty mug on the draining board and grabbed her jacket and keys.

'Can I do something for you, on my last day here?' He called after her, as she headed for the front door.

Dani paused. 'It's a Wednesday. I know it sounds weird, but can you spend lunchtime at the St Enoch Centre? You can buy me a parting gift if you like. It's the time and day when Maisie used to hang around there. I don't know what I think you might find – but it's worth a try.'

'I'll do it,' he shouted back, blowing a kiss to her retreating form.

*

Andy knocked on the office door, watching for Dani to wave him in. When he took the seat across the desk from her, he thought she looked pre-occupied.

'I hope you don't mind,' he began sheepishly. 'I've

been chasing up a lead I got from one of the members of the Storm.'

'The letters that might have been written by Maisie, you mean?' Dani became suddenly alert.

Andy placed the package on the desk in front of her. 'She's using the name Kenna Adams. Fiona's maiden name was Adams and the stuff she writes about very closely follows the events of Maisie's life.'

'Fine,' she said impatiently. 'But does it actually get us anywhere?'

'I think it does. In these letters, Maisie discusses her parents' divorce and her father's move to Norway. Where they really get interesting is when she talks about Charles' new wife. Maisie claims the woman only married her father to gain insider information about his company. She accuses her step-mother of being a spy for an environmental action group.'

'Bloody hell, we need to check this out, straight away.'

'I already have.'

Dani stared at him oddly, but said nothing.

'Magda Hustad questioned Andreas Nilsen again. Kristin Berg attended the same university as him. The man admitted that Kristin took the job at Barents Oil so she could gather information for him.'

'How long have you known this?' Her voice sounded hollow.

'Only since last evening, when Magda called me back.'

'Okay, so is the marriage just a sham – what about the child?'

'Andreas claims that Kristin genuinely fell in love with Charles, it wasn't part of the plan. Before that, she'd been in a relationship with him. He was heartbroken when she married the guy.'

'So Maisie knew that Kristin had been a member

of this organisation. Did she tell her father? Is Charles aware of all this?'

'I don't think so, do you? I saw no sign of it when they were together.'

Dani sat back in her seat, considering this new information. 'We should tell Dieter, find out what his take on it is.'

Andy pursed his lips. 'I don't see it's got much to do with him.'

'The snatching of the Riddell's boy was *his* case. This puts it in a new light. What if Kristin orchestrated the whole thing to frighten her husband?'

'That assumes Kristin is still working for Nilsen and I don't really think she is. I can't see her having a baby with Charles purely for the sake of their environmental campaign. It would be incredibly mercenary.'

'I still believe that Dieter has a right to know. Why didn't Magda try to contact him and let the guy in on what was happening? Why didn't you inform me *before* you called Norway, for that matter?'

Andy took a very deep breath, not wanting to end up in an argument with her. 'Magda has been trying to get hold of Karlsen for days. She's got no idea where he is. Apparently, some Inspector from the Chief's office is sniffing around their cold cases. Magda's got herself into a state about it. God knows what the pair of them have been up to.'

'Did you tell her he was here in Glasgow?'

'I didn't think that was my place, Ma'am.'

'Why have you kept all this to yourself, Andy?' She leant forward and rested her steely eyes upon him.

'Because all I signed up for in this job was to solve crimes, not clear up the mess created by your bloody love life.' As soon as the words were out,

Andy regretted them, not because they weren't true but because Dani appeared so stricken that he'd said them her face had crumpled and her eyes were filling up.

'Get out,' she hissed levelly.

He quickly did as Dani said, knowing that as soon as he'd left the poky wee office, his friend would let the tears fall.

*

When the DCI's phone buzzed a couple of hours later she was tempted to ignore it. Seeing it was Dieter, she fought back a sob and took the call. 'Hi.'

'Hey, Dani. Can you come down to the St Enoch Centre right now? There's something I need you to see.'

'Is it urgent?'

'I think so.'

'Okay, I'll be there in ten minutes. I'll call you when I arrive.'

The traffic was busy and it was more like half an hour before Dani reached the shopping precinct. She spotted Dieter's tall frame leaning against a post at the bottom of an escalator. He bent down and gave her a deep kiss. 'You're just in time,' he said.

Dani crinkled her brow in puzzlement.

The Norwegian flicked his head towards a pizza restaurant just opposite them. 'Do you see the couple sitting by the window? I've been watching them for an hour or so. You asked me to look out for anything unusual. I spent a lot of time examining the Maisie Riddell case files back at the Bureau. I'm fairly sure that woman is Maisie's mother.'

Dani took a pace nearer. 'You're right, and the guy having lunch with her is my Sergeant, Phil Boag.' The DCI kept walking towards the restaurant, with Dieter following close behind. She pushed through the doors and marched straight up to the table.

Phil glanced up from his plate. 'Ma'am?'

'Do you mind if we join you?'

They both shook their heads, shifting along the booth so that Dani and Dieter could sit at opposite sides.

'I can explain,' Phil began awkwardly. 'Fiona and I haven't seen each other socially since the day Maisie went missing, but she found out I'd been suspended from duty and wanted to talk to me.'

'We decided to meet at the same place and time we always used to, especially if it was going to be the last opportunity to see one another,' Fiona continued. 'I wanted to give Phil some moral support. I knew he'd be going through a rough few days.'

'So is this where you met on a weekly basis, for the last year or so?' Dani looked at them both in turn.

'Yes, unless it was too busy in here, then we went to the burger bar across the way,' Fiona clarified.

'But this was where Maisie was coming to, each Wednesday lunchtime, when she bunked off school. She'd hang around the shops and buy herself some lunch. Maisie *must* have seen the two of you here on at least one of those occasions. Didn't you make the connection, Phil?'

DS Boag appeared confused. 'I didn't think about it. The city centre is a big place, we were always very careful not to be followed here.'

'Not careful enough,' Dani said dryly.

'So Maisie knew all about my affair with Phil?' Fiona looked horrified. She buried her face in her hands and began to cry. 'No wonder she ran away! Why didn't she just talk to me about it?'

Phil leant across the dirty plates and clasped her

hands tightly. 'You mustn't blame yourself darling, it wasn't your fault.'

Dani slid out of the seat and tapped Dieter on the shoulder, indicating they should leave the pair to it. The couple proceeded out into the mall, dodging the little clusters of shoppers milling past, finding a quiet spot, well away from the restaurant.

'So that was why Maisie took off. She thought her mother was about to destroy her best friend's family. Added to that, Maisie hated her dad's new wife, believing their life to be a total sham.' Dani looked Dieter in the eye. 'Maybe she'd finally decided it was time to fight back.'

Chapter Thirty Five

Joy Hutchison was taking a fine art course at Falkirk College. The lessons were every Wednesday evening. Tonight, the group would be studying the use of perspective. Joy hoped it would give her some tips on how to proceed with the landscape drawing that she had come to love so much.

Bill was busy upstairs in the spare room when she departed. Sam Sharpe had gone out ten minutes earlier, so she left through the front door without any fanfare. Joy thought she'd probably be back before her husband even noticed his wife had gone. *He* was more interested in their son's old trainset than the grandchildren were.

The lamp in the spare room where Bill kept his model railway was fitted with a low wattage bulb. A couple of the trains had little headlamps attached to them and he enjoyed watching them whiz around the track in the semi-darkness. Bill had joined a local owner's club and a week ago he managed to get hold of a moulded hillside which fitted over the rails and allowed the trains to fly through a short tunnel system. He was sure his grandsons would particularly like this new addition to the set.

He found pottering around with these pieces very therapeutic. Seeing the set all together again made him think about his son. Joy and Bill had lost Neil when he was only ten years old, in a hill walking accident. It had taken a long time for them to get over the tragedy. Bill had reacted particularly badly to Neil's death and suffered a nervous breakdown not long afterwards. Only very recently had the couple learnt to put their pain aside and concentrate more on their daughter and her two boys. The new friendship he had forged with DCI Bevan had also been useful in his recovery. They seemed to view the world in a similar way, or Bill had thought so until recently. In the last few weeks he'd found the detective distant and lacking her usual sympathy for the plight of others. Perhaps it was simply this new case she was working on. The disappearance of a child was a harrowing thing to have to investigate.

Bill was leaning across to adjust a set of points when he heard a noise downstairs. He wondered if it was Joy, getting ready for her evening class in town. Then he spotted his Flying Scotsman. He picked it up and examined the glossy blue paintwork with pride, remembering Neil's excited face when he'd opened up the box on Christmas morning and held it in his small hands, all those years ago.

The old man allowed himself to drift off into this pleasant memory, feeling the satisfying weight of the engine in his palm. Suddenly, he sensed a movement behind him. Something compelled him to shift to one side. As he did so, a large, dark form lunged forward, gripping at his arm and upsetting the table upon which the railway was delicately placed. The model engines and track fell to the floor with a clatter, which seemed to distract Bill's attacker for a split second.

In this second, Bill had time to turn. He saw a man, dressed entirely in black, his face obscured by some kind of mask, looming over him with a long hunting blade. Bill found he still had the heavy engine in his hand and automatically held it up to defend himself against the knife, which he could see was being swiped downwards towards his throat. Bill sent up an arm, immediately feeling the stinging pain of the sharp blade on his skin.

He knew there was no chance of rebuffing another attack, but he held up his arms defensively nonetheless, bracing himself for the worst. Then the man stumbled. Bill could tell he'd been struck from behind, because the dark figure collapsed forwards and Bill had to duck out of the way so as not to be crushed by his falling body.

*

An eerie silence followed, which seemed to last for some time, although in reality it must have been less than a moment or two. Sam Sharpe was trying to manoeuvre Bill out of the room. He looked downwards and saw blood everywhere, streaked down his trousers and leaving a trail on the floor. The American led his friend into a bedroom where he pulled the sheet off the bed. He ripped it into a long strip and proceeded to wind it tightly around Bill's upper arm. He tied it up and fumbled for his mobile phone, demanding the police and an ambulance in a tone that Bill thought was barely controlled. Once Sam had ended the call, they heard Joy coming back in through the front door.

Chapter Thirty Six

It was in the early hours of the morning that Dani received the call. She took a quick shower and got dressed. The DCI rested her weight on the edge of the bed and placed a hand on Dieter's shoulder, gently shaking him awake. He gazed at her with sleepy eyes.

'Something's happened. I'm not going to be able to come with you to the airport.'

Dieter shifted up, putting his arms around her. 'Is everything okay? You look pale.'

'A friend of mine is in hospital, he's been attacked. I wouldn't leave you otherwise.'

He pulled Dani closer, kissing her passionately and cupping her face in his hands. 'I'll call you as soon as I've landed.'

The Detective sensed a lump forming in her throat. She couldn't trust herself to speak so she simply nodded, rising up and leaving the hot, musty room, pulling the door shut behind her, knowing it was important that she keep moving forward and not look back.

Bill Hutchison had a bed in the general ward of Falkirk Hospital. Joy was sitting in the chair next to him, reading a paperback novel, whilst Bill dozed peacefully. Dani had managed to get hold of a bunch of flowers on her way over, but as she laid them on the plain covers, they looked a little shabby.

Joy put down her book and rose to greet her friend, placing a kiss on her cheek. 'DCI Bevan! What a relief to see you, thanks for coming.'

Dani kept hold of the lady's hands, glancing at Bill's sleeping form. 'Tell me what happened.'

'He came for Bill - Richard Erskine, I mean. The man must have been watching the house and knew I'd gone out for my evening class. He broke in through the back door and crept up the stairs to where Bill was working on the train set. He had a knife, Dani.' Joy had a horrified expression on her face.

'How on earth did Bill manage to fight him off?' Dani knew that Erskine moved swiftly and without mercy, attacking his victims from behind and taking them unawares.

'He heard a movement in the doorway and shifted to the side. This put Erskine off balance when he went to strike. The table became upturned in the commotion and the train set fell to the floor. Bill was able to put up his arms to defend himself. That was when he sustained the wounds. He's had twelve stitches in his right arm and they needed to give him a blood transfusion, that's why he's so weak.'

Dani still didn't understand how Bill survived, but she allowed Joy to show her a beautifully crafted little engine that was sitting on the bedside table. 'Bill had this is his hand when he fought off Erskine's blows.'

The detective looked at it closely, observing the deep score that had been etched into the otherwise glossy paintwork.

'It had been Neil's favourite.'

Dani wondered if this was supposed to be the explanation for Bill's miraculous escape from death. But then her questions were answered when she heard a familiar voice behind her.

'Hello Dani.'

She turned slowly, taking in the strangely welcome sight of Sam Sharpe, looking as if he'd been up all night and needed a wash and a shave. 'Hi Sam.'

'Can we talk?' He asked cautiously. 'There's a café on the floor below.'

They left Joy by her husband's bedside and took the lift down to the cafeteria, neither of them saying much during the short journey. Sam bought the coffees and Dani bagged them a table in the corner.

'I should really explain,' the American said awkwardly.

'Go ahead.'

'Bill called me in the States a few days ago. He needed my help. You were wrapped up in your missing girl case and when he suggested that Erskine might be involved in his investigations I knew I had to come over.'

The penny suddenly dropped. 'Did you help Bill to uncover the prostitution racket and get the girl out of that place?'

He nodded. 'I only provided back-up. Bill was the one who led the operation.'

'You make it sound like something legitimate.' Dani sipped the coffee, which was actually quite good.

'I wasn't keen on the idea, but Bill had evidence from Sinclair's wife that underage girls were being sexually exploited in the building. Bill felt that you and DI Lyons weren't giving him a fair hearing, so he decided to go it alone.'

'What happened last night?'

'I'd popped into town to get a bottle of wine to replenish the Hutchisons' drinks cabinet. When I came back into the house, about forty minutes later, I saw the glass in the back door had been broken. An almighty crash came from upstairs. I bolted up there, just as this guy in a black mask was lunging at Bill with a huge knife. I grabbed for the lamp on the table and struck him hard on the back of the head with the ceramic base. The attacker fell forwards and that's when I saw the blood. Bill had been slashed on the arm and it was bleeding badly. My first instinct was to get him out of there and stem the flow. We went into the guest room and I used my sheet as a tourniquet. I called the cops and then Joy came back.'

'What about Erskine?' Dani sat on the edge of her seat, holding her breath.

Sam looked uncomfortable. 'I was busy getting Bill patched up and then calming Joy down. I fixed the couple a brandy in the sitting room and quickly jogged back up to the study. When I got there, he was gone.'

'How could he be gone?'

'I suppose he must have been dazed by the blow to his head and when he came to, realised there were more people in the house and made a run for it. The police think he might have gone out of the study window and onto the garage roof. They're still processing the forensics on it. He'd left the knife behind. It was dripping with blood, but it would all have been Bill's. The man wore gloves, so I don't expect for a second there were any prints on it.' Sam looked down at his cup. 'I'm sorry he got away.'

'Without you, Bill would be dead. I would be visiting one of Erskine's blood-chilling crime scenes and it would be *Bill* positioned there with his throat cut.' Dani thought for a moment. 'Why did Erskine target him in the first place?'

'I reckon Erskine's been casing this Fisherman's Bar for weeks, the landlady said there'd been some new faces hanging around and asking questions. That's how he found out about Sinclair's involvement. Erskine must have thought that Bill was mixed up in it too. He'd been talking to the landlady a lot and then, the other night, Erskine must have been there. He must have seen Bill going up those stairs and assumed he was a customer, or even one of the ring-leaders.'

'So that was why Erskine was watching the Hutchisons' property. He'd seen Bill hanging around with Sinclair's associates at the Fisherman's Bar and ear-marked him as a target.'

'At least DI Lyons is now on side. He's prepared to see Richard Erskine as their prime suspect.'

Dani briefly outlined for Sam the details of Clive Anton's murder in Glasgow. 'I'll need to call DI Jilly Reid and tell her to liaise with Lyons, so they can tie the two investigations together.'

Sam leant forward and brushed his fingers against Dani's cheek. 'This time Erskine's made a mistake, he's never done that before. The guy's got a head injury, he lost consciousness for a little while at least. He must be covered in Bill's blood and he didn't have the opportunity to change his clothes at the scene, like he usually does. Maybe they'll be able to do a trace on the knife. There's going to be evidence with this one. The cops are bound to catch him.'

'I sincerely hope you're right.'

Sam smiled. 'Are you okay? You look really well.'

Dani cleared her throat. 'Why didn't you call me and say you were in the country?'

'We hadn't arranged anything and I knew you were in the middle of a biggie. I didn't want to put pressure on you. I did leave some messages.'

'I got them. I've just been busy, that's all.' Dani did her best to avoid eye contact.

Sam took her hand and she felt herself squirm with embarrassment and shame. 'Tell me Dani, would you have wanted me to call you as soon as I arrived, and let you know that I was here?'

She kept her gazed fixed on the table top, slowly shaking her head from side to side. 'No, I wouldn't have.'

Sam snatched his hand back. 'That's all I needed to know.'

Chapter Thirty Seven

The doctors reassured Dani that Bill was perfectly stable, so she returned to Glasgow later that afternoon. The DCI went straight to the office, not wishing to see her flat just yet; where she would be reminded of Dieter's absence.

Fortunately, Andy was not at his desk. Bevan wasn't sure what to say to him. She needed some space to think first. As soon as she'd closed the door, Dani reached for the package which contained the letters from Kenna Adams. In order to try and second guess Maisie's actions, the detective decided to get inside the girl's head. She placed her take-out cup of coffee within reach and began to read.

The teenager's musings about her step-mother seemed to teeter between fantasy and reality. Kristin was depicted in these letters like an ice-queen in a child's fairy story. She had bewitched her new husband and manipulated his thoughts and actions. Kenna described how Kristin gathered intimate details about the family and then reported them back to the faceless, wicked organisation for which she worked.

Dani imagined that Maisie had discovered how her step-mother originally joined Barents Oil in order to sabotage their work. She must have assumed that Kristin took this role to the extreme by marrying her father and giving him a new child. If Maisie already resented the woman, this fact must have fuelled her hatred. Then, over the last few months, Maisie found out her mother was sleeping with Phil. Dani could picture how confused and let-down the adolescent must have felt.

Maisie had been singing in various clubs and hoarding the money she made from this. She also had the savings that her Dad deposited for her in the building society. This would give her the funds she needed to take action. But what was Maisie planning to do? Dani took a sip of her cappuccino. Perhaps she met someone in one of these clubs who promised to get her over to Scandinavia. They may have offered to produce false travel documents, all of which would require cash.

The DCI felt certain that Maisie was headed to Norway. She was spotted on the docks at Newcastle on the Thursday night after she disappeared. There'd been no further sightings of her in the UK since. Dani was convinced she found passage to the continent.

So what was the girl planning? Bevan had a suspicion that Maisie was intent on unmasking Kristin Riddell and proving to her father that he'd married the wrong person. How she was intending to do this, Dani didn't know. She suddenly longed to talk it through with Andy, who understood the case just as well as she did.

To progress with the investigation, the DCI knew she had to return to Norway. The answer to Maisie's disappearance lay there, she was certain. Of course she wanted to see Dieter again, but was sure that this desire wasn't affecting her judgement in any way. Bevan would just need to speak with the DCS and try to persuade him that it was a good idea.

*

A lady taking her dog for a walk let Dani in through the communal entrance door. She climbed the wide, carpeted stairway to the first floor, breathed in deeply and gave a gentle knock.

It was Carol who answered, looking surprised. 'DCI Bevan, please come in.'

'Call me Dani.' She stepped over the threshold. 'Sorry to bother you in the evening. I needed to have a word with Andy.'

Carol turned down the heat under a pot on the stove and left Dani in the small but modern kitchen. A couple of minutes later, Andy came through the door, dressed in a T-shirt and jogging pants.

'Ma'am? Has something come up?'

'Take a seat. I wanted to have a chat.'

The DC did as he was told, but his expression remained impassive. He was obviously going to let her do the talking.

'I didn't want to leave things as they were yesterday. We need to work together for the sake of the case.'

'Of course. The investigation is my priority.'

Dani knew he was implying that it might not be hers, but she decided to let this go, in the interests of détente. 'I've been reading through those letters you gave me. I'm convinced that Maisie had devised some kind of plan to prove what Kristin was up to. I want to go back to Stavanger in order to find out more. Andy, I need you to come with me. I can't solve this thing without you.' She placed her hands palm up on the table, in a gesture of openness.

He narrowed his eyes. 'If this scheme is all about providing you with an opportunity to see your boyfriend again, I'm not willing to leave Carol and Amy on that basis.'

'It isn't.' Dani was determined not to rise to the bait. 'But if you were to wear one of your festive jumpers, that would be an added bonus.'

Andy finally cracked a smile. 'Fine. Is the DCS okay with us flying out there for a second time?'

'The discovery that Kristin Riddell was embroiled with this environmentalist group gives us the justification to question the family again. Nicholson couldn't argue with that. If you can pack a bag tonight, I'll book us a flight for the morning.'

It was now early April and there was a definite hint of spring in the air. On this visit to Norway, the British detectives were determined to lead their own investigation, not to rely upon the Bureau to guide them.

Dani had booked a couple of rooms in a guesthouse positioned in the historical centre of Stavanger. She felt they'd gain a far better feel for the place from here. The DCI gazed out of the window of her neat little room and spotted the tea shop across the market square, where she and Sophie Karlsen had discussed the assault on Aron Holm.

As soon as they'd deposited their bags and freshened up, Andy knocked on her door. He'd booked a taxi to take them out to the Riddells' place. After a couple of kilometres of silence Calder said, 'are you going to tell Dieter that you're here?'

'This is police business, not a holiday. I owe it to Maisie to keep focussed.'

'Good. I think that's wise,' Andy commented with feeling.

The taxi drove down the bumpy track towards the isolated house. Dani asked the driver to return for them in half an hour. There were no cars parked outside. The detectives hoped someone was at home.

It was Kristin who opened up. Her thin body gave a physical jolt when she saw them standing on the doorstep. 'Charles isn't here, he's at the office,' she said quickly.

'Can we come in?' Dani was already halfway

across the threshold.

Kristin led the way into the open-plan lounge. Gabriel was noisily stacking bricks on the coffee table. 'Why have you come back?' Her voice was fearful.

'We've learnt some new facts, Mrs Riddell. We believe they may have a strong bearing on the case.'

Kristin sat on the sofa and put her head in her hands.

'Have you heard from Maisie since she went missing?' Andy asked.

Kristin raised her eyes to glare at him. 'Of course not! I would have told the police if I had. My husband is going out of his mind with worry.'

The detectives sat on the sofa opposite her. 'Maisie possessed some information about you, Kristin. Were you aware of that?' Andy observed her levelly, thinking she looked depressed.

'I suspected she might.' Her voice was a whisper.

'Did you ever confront your step-daughter about what she knew?'

'I assume you are talking about my historic involvement with Andreas Nilsen and his organisation. No, I never spoke with Maisie about it. The girl hated me. Even if I told her it was all in the past she would not have believed it.'

'Do you think Maisie informed your husband?'

'I don't think she did. It gave her greater pleasure to keep me in suspense. Maisie liked to know that she held my future happiness in the palm of her hand.'

'It provides you with a perfect motive to want Maisie out of the way,' Dani said quietly.

'Yes, I suppose it does. But I never did anything to her. I'm an environmentalist and a mother. I fell in love with someone I shouldn't. I'm not a murderer.' The woman settled her clear blue eyes upon Dani's face. The DCI was inclined to believe her. Besides, they knew Kristin was in Stavanger on the day Maisie went missing.

'Listen, Kristin. We're here because we want you to do us a favour.'

The woman looked puzzled.

'We think Maisie left Glasgow to come here. We have a sighting of her attempting to get on a boat to Amsterdam. She may still be making her way to Norway, or she may already be in the area.'

'What is she here to do?' Kristin automatically put a hand up to her collar and pulled her little boy closer.

'We believe Maisie is trying to gather evidence against you, so that when she confronts your husband, he cannot refute her claims.'

Kristin had tears in her eyes. She glanced through the tall glass windows at the dark trees which encircled the house. 'I don't want to stay here any longer.'

'I can understand that,' Dani continued. 'But I don't think Maisie is going to hurt you or your son. What she may do is try to contact Charles. The girl might already have done so. Could you keep a close eye on all the mail and phone calls you receive? If you notice anything unusual, then please give me a call.' Dani handed the woman her card.

She nodded, tears streaming down her face. 'I always wanted to tell him. But the longer time goes by, the harder it is, you know?'

Dani placed a hand on her shoulder. 'Try not to worry Kristin. We'll get this resolved, I promise.'

*

Andy chose a small local restaurant for them to eat in. He'd finally got over the inexplicable rage he'd felt at seeing his boss with Dieter Karlsen and decided to mend some bridges. They ordered French wine but wanted to try some typical Norwegian food. Dani ordered the salted cod and Andy went for a mutton stew which the menu claimed was the national dish. The meal proved to be hearty and warming. The pair began to relax as they worked their way through a very good bottle of Bordeaux.

'Are you sure the assault on Aron Holm is unrelated to this business with Kristin Riddell?' Andy sipped his wine thoughtfully.

'Completely. The Bureau cleared Andreas Nilsen of any involvement in the attack.'

'Magda said Nilsen was very supportive of Aron Holm's work. He claimed he hoped the scientist would be successful and this would mean his campaign was no longer necessary. It just got me thinking, that perhaps we've looked at this the wrong way round. It wouldn't have been the *environmentalists* who wanted to stop Holm's research, but the oil industry itself.'

'But it was Skaldic Conglomerates who were funding Holm's work. I've told you, it's just a blind alley.' Dani poured out the last of the wine between their glasses.

'You seem very sure,' Andy said innocently, wiping up the remainder of his stew with a slice of bread. 'We usually keep an open mind on these things.'

Dani was relieved when the mobile phone in her pocket started to buzz. She excused herself and stepped outside to take the call, the fresh air making her feel suddenly tipsy.

'Dani? I really didn't want to bother you again but I thought you'd like to know the latest.'

'Sam, it's good to hear from you. How is Bill doing?'

'He's fine. Joy will be taking him home tomorrow.

I said I'd help to get him settled back in, until their daughter comes down in a few days.'

'Great, they're really lucky to have you with them.'

'There was a witness. One of the Hutchisons' neighbours saw Erskine's car speeding away from the scene, on the night of the attack. It was a pretty unusual sight on that quiet estate and the man wrote down the number plate. It was enough for DI Lyons to get a warrant to search his house in Inverness. The guy hadn't had time to get rid of much. They found some bloody trainers and seized his laptop. Erskine had been using the computer to track down his targets. There were loads of searches on Sinclair and Anton. It's circumstantial, but with the forensics they should be able to build a solid case. This time, I really think they've got him.'

'Oh, Sam, I'm so pleased. I know how important it was to you to see the man brought to justice.'

'Yeah, it's good news.' There was an awkward silence before Sam grunted a farewell and ended the call.

Dani was left standing in the crisp cold, looking out into the busy square, with its old fashioned street lights providing a warm glow, wondering if she'd done the right thing after all.

Chapter Thirty Nine

Dc Alice Mann gazed around the near empty floor of the Serious Crime Division, before resting her eyes upon her colleague sitting opposite.

'How come Andy Calder always accompanies the DCI on these trips?' She enquired of him.

'Because he's got the most experience and Bevan's worked with him for years,' Dan Clifton replied reasonably.

'I don't know why she lets him get away with speaking to her the way he does. Sometimes in briefings, it's like he's openly taking the piss. If you or I did that, we'd be off the force.'

'Andy's had a difficult time these last few years. You know he suffered a massive heart attack, just before his wife had the baby? It was the boss who saved his life. I suppose that creates a bond between them.'

'Yeah, I get that. But the rest of us have stuff to offer too, you know? But Calder kind of bullies us down, so there's no other view but his.'

'I think that's a bit strong. Andy's a good bloke.'

Alice said nothing, imagining Dan and the other male DCs down at the pub with Andy, exchanging jokes and slapping each other on the back. She shook the image out of her head, turning instead to the line of inquiry she was currently investigating.

After their trip to the Port of Tyne, Alice had been examining maps of the Northumberland coast, trying to identify another place where the group of illegals Maisie had joined could have gained passage across the North Sea.

There were several shipping ports along that particular coastline, notably at the mouth of the River Tyne. Mann was assuming the gang had transport, in which case they could have tried any of the docks within a thirty mile radius, from South Shields down to Sunderland. The search parameters were huge and only she and Dan were working on it. She sighed heavily, trying to shift herself into the mindset of someone attempting to smuggle people out of the country illegally. In reality, ports were dangerous places for criminals. They were full of security cameras and customs officials. If the group had no joy at the Port of Tyne, perhaps they changed tack slightly.

Alice looked back at her map, running her finger along the jagged coast towards the north of the county. 'How well do you know Northumberland, Dan?' she called across the desk, without glancing up.

'I'm from Sheffield, but I know it a little bit. We went on holiday to Alnwick once.'

'What about the coast, do you know of any little shipping towns, or ports up there - somewhere that's smaller than the more obvious places to the south?' Alice eyed her friend closely.

Dan stood up and walked around the desk. He bent over the map and spent a few minutes examining it. 'Whitley Bay, Blyth and Amble are all fishing villages, I think.'

'How do you fancy another jaunt over the border?' She raised her eyebrows playfully.

'As long as we square it with the boss, I'm up for it, yeah.'

*

'If Maisie were trying to gather evidence against her step-mother, where would she start?' Dani asked her colleague, as she tucked into a breakfast of coffee and pastries, thinking out loud.

'I'd suggest she'd begin with what she already knew. Maisie had found out Kristin was in the environmentalist movement when she was at university. I think she might have gone there to find out more.'

'I agree. It's the kind of place where a fourteen year old, who looked older than her years, might blend in unnoticed.'

The University of Stavanger was based in an unassuming grey building that reminded Dani, strangely, of Newton High School. The detectives spoke briefly with the principal, who had allowed them to spend time in the student recreational areas, asking questions. Both officers had photographs of Maisie, which they were showing to as many people as possible.

By lunchtime, it was clear that they weren't going to have much luck from the student body; nobody appeared to have seen the girl. Bevan decided to try the Environmental Sciences Department, where both Andreas Nilsen and Kristin Berg had been undergraduates.

The Department was based along a corridor on the top floor of the building. They examined the names on the office doors, stopping at the one which seemed to be the most senior. Professor Nils Holgren called out something in Norwegian that the detectives took as an invitation to enter.

The office was lined with books and the man had an impressive view out of the window behind his desk. On this sunny day, the light was putting the man's face in shadow, although Dani could tell he was well into his fifties.

'My name is Detective Chief Inspector Bevan, we are here from Glasgow. I wonder if we could ask you a few questions, Professor?'

The man said nothing, gesturing towards the chairs in front of his desk and shifting forward slightly, thankfully moving him into a better light. 'What can I do to help?'

'Have you worked at the university long?' Andy asked bluntly, clearly not wishing to waste any time.

'Twenty five years next month,' he answered proudly. 'I shall retire at the end of the summer.'

'Do you recall a couple of students who studied in your department, their names were Andreas Nilsen and Kristin Berg?'

'What is this regarding?' The man enquired cautiously.

'We are investigating the disappearance of this girl,' Dani placed the photograph on the desk in front of him. 'She is Kristin Berg's step-daughter. Our investigations have led us to examine Kristin's involvement in an environmental organisation when she was a student, the one which Andreas Nilsen set up.'

The man made a steeple out of his hands, revealing a thick gold wedding band on his veiny finger. 'Well, I might hesitate to say it was Andreas who established the Environmental Liberation Group. It has been operating for many years. But I suppose he is currently the most active member.'

'Do you know much about this group then,' Dani pressed.

'I take a very keen interest in all environmental issues which affect this city. I've lived here all my life.'

'Did you know Kristin Berg?'

'Oh yes, she was a very lovely girl and caused a great stir amongst the other students when she was here. Kristin was also very fired up about preserving the beauty of Norway's natural environment.'

'Would it surprise you to learn that Kristin is now married to Charles Riddell, one of the Chief Executives of Barents Oil?'

If the man was surprised he didn't show it. 'Was that Andreas' idea? He always was a little *over enthusiastic*.'

'It was Andreas who suggested she take a job as Riddell's secretary, but Kristin claims she fell in love with her boss. They now have a baby son.'

Hilgren nodded slowly. 'Life is complicated like that. I expect Andreas took it very badly, but it was inevitable. When two people work so closely together and one happens to be very beautiful, what else can the boy have expected?'

Dani was surprised by the Professor's insight. 'Do you support the aims of the Environmental Liberation Group?'

Hilgren smiled ruefully. 'In my job I cannot be seen to have a political axe to grind. All I can say is that I take a keen interest in their campaigns.'

Andy leant forward. 'Have you heard of a scientist called Aron Holm?'

This time, Hilgren did seem taken aback. 'Aron and I studied together, many years ago. I've followed his research very carefully ever since.'

'Did you hear he was badly assaulted eighteen months back? He spent a while in hospital as a result.'

Dani wondered where Andy was going with this, but to have closed down the questioning would have seemed suspicious.

'Yes, I heard about it. My wife and I sent flowers to him. It was an awful thing to have happened. I was very pleased that Aron still carried on with his work afterwards, he was never one to be intimidated.'

'So you believe he was attacked by somebody who wasn't happy about Holm's research into an alternative to crude oil?' Andy's interest had been piqued.

'Well, it would have been an incredible coincidence if that wasn't the case. I'm not a great believer in conspiracy theories, detective. I am always warning my students against subscribing to them. But in incidences such as the assault on Aron Holm, one would have to be incredibly naïve to assume it wasn't an attempt to prevent his research from continuing.'

'The police looked into the assault and found nothing. Even Holm himself told us he thought it was a case of mistaken identity,' Dani quickly put-in.

Andy flashed her a suspicious glance.

Hilgren let out a disapproving grunt. 'There are members of the police force who are in the pockets of the oil industry, I'm afraid. As for Holm, he has always been an idealist, with his head in the clouds. Aron wouldn't be able to contemplate that there are people who would want to obstruct work which is aimed at serving the greater good. Sadly, *we* know better.'

'Yes, we certainly do,' Andy replied decisively, before his boss could say anything at all to the contrary.

Chapter Forty

Having drawn a blank with their investigations in the seaside town of Whitley Bay, DC Clifton drove further up the coast to Blyth. Alice gazed out of the window at the attractive countryside passing by. The day had been a mixture of sunshine and showers, but it felt good to be next to the sea.

Alice Mann had grown up in Largs, a pretty place on the Firth of Clyde, with magnificent views of the hills of Arran and Bute across the water. Her parents were well into their forties when she was born and Alice remained an only child. Her home had been a quiet and unexciting one, where books took precedence over real life experiences. As soon as Alice graduated from university, she craved the challenge that a career in the police force would bring. She knew her parents were secretly horrified by her decision to join the police graduate programme. They had slowly come around to accepting her new lifestyle. Although, she suspected that her mum and dad worried about her a great deal.

Alice had bought herself a travel guide in one of the service stations on the way down. She discovered that Blyth was a town which once had a burgeoning shipbuilding industry. It had long since gone into decline but the docks were still thriving, largely because of the shipping of paper from Scandinavia, which was used in the newspaper trades of England and Scotland. This knowledge had given Mann a flicker of hope that this was a place where a boat may have set sail for Norway.

Dan Clifton guided the car slowly through the town centre, heading for the docks. As they approached the quayside and scanned the roads for parking spaces, Alice caught sight of several huge wind turbines, on the opposite side of the river, looming ominously over the town. The detective imagined they must be visible from miles out to sea. She wondered if Maisie had seen them on the night she tried to find a boat to take her to her father. Alice thought how terrified the girl would have felt and how her resolve must surely have been tested by the idea of the terrible voyage which lay ahead.

Dan had parked by the harbour wall. The pair got out of the car and pulled their jackets up to their ears, the cold northerly wind making their faces turn immediately numb. They strode towards the commercial docks first, asking questions at the offices of several shipping firms, all of whom denied seeing the rag-tag band of individuals who were desperately trying to leave the country that night.

As they strolled back past the harbour, Alice suggested they try the owners of the myriad fishing boats tied up at the moorings down there. Dan remained sceptical, but they'd come all this way and it made sense to be methodical. Quite a few of the boats were in. It was getting late in the day and the wind was gusting fiercely. Waves had begun to swirl into the semi-circular harbour, licking up at the stone wall which enclosed it.

A man in a bright orange life jacket was carrying plastic trays filled with fish onto the landing stage next to his boat. The vessel was rising and falling in the strengthening swell. 'Excuse me,' Alice called over, holding up her warrant card. 'May we ask you a couple of questions?'

The man nodded. 'Just give me a minute to get my catch onto dry land.'

As they drew close, the smell of raw fish was extremely potent. Alice could see that Dan was scrunching up his face in distaste, but she actually rather liked it. So when the fisherman finally finished hauling the pallets out of the hull of the boat and held out his hand, she didn't hesitate to take it.

'I'm Mick Burdis. What can I do for you?'

'My name is DC Mann and this is my colleague, DC Clifton. We are investigating the disappearance of this girl.' Alice handed him the photo.

He looked at it carefully. 'I really don't recognise her from round here. She's the lass who went missing from Glasgow, is that right? What makes you think she'd made it down to these parts?'

'There was a possible sighting, at the Port of Tyne. We think she was part of a group trying to gain illegal passage on one of the boats sailing to Scandinavia.'

'It wouldn't be easy these days. Cargo is very carefully monitored. It wouldn't be worth a skipper's while to take anything illegal on board, unless it was particularly lucrative. What night was this sighting?'

'The evening of Thursday the nineteenth.'

The dark-haired man paused and then said, 'come aboard for a second. I'll take a look in my log and see if anything unusual went on that night.'

The detectives followed him onto the tilting boat, with Dan nearly losing his footing on the slippery deck. They stepped into the wheelhouse and waited, whilst Mick scanned a shelf full of notebooks and directories. 'Here we go,' he flicked through the dog-eared pages, until alighting on the correct entry. 'Aye, I thought that was the same evening.' He looked up. 'There was a storm on the nineteenth, out in the sea at about 9.30pm. The lighthouse at Whitley Bay activated the fog horn and the docks went to red alert. My son works on one of the ships over there. It was a bad night, he said.'

'Did any boats actually set sail on that evening then?' Dan asked in near frustration.

Mick thought about it. 'I'll tell you who I've not seen since that day, Tony Howey. He's got a fishing trawler and it's usually moored here until the spring. It's a fairly sturdy boat and he's got a permanent crew of three or four. If I'm honest, I'd not given it a second thought that he hadn't been around. I don't like him very much, so I suppose I was relieved not to have to speak with him.'

'Does this man have any family nearby?'

'I think he lives in the town, sure. But whether he has a wife or kids, I couldn't tell you.'

'Thank you very much for your help,' DC Clifton said decisively, making a move back up top, his face beginning to turn a sickly shade of pale green.

Alice stayed for a moment and shook the man's hand once again. 'We really appreciate this information, Sir. I've got a feeling it's going to prove very important.'

Chapter Forty One

It was the middle of the night when Bevan's mobile phone began to buzz insistently on the bedside table. Being woken so abruptly was disorientating and it took her a moment to recall that she was in the guesthouse in Stavanger.

'DCI Bevan, is that you?'

Dani composed herself and replied. 'Yes, this is Bevan.'

'It's Kristin Riddell,' the woman was speaking in a kind of strangulated whisper. 'She's outside now! Maisie is coming to get us!'

'Calm down, Mrs Riddell. Please tell me what's happening.' Dani used her most soothing voice, glancing at her watch and seeing it was 3am. She ran a hand despairingly through her cropped hair.

'I woke up about ten minutes ago, I didn't know why exactly, but I thought it might have been because Gabriel had cried out for me. I got up and went into his room. That's when I saw her – she had her face pressed up to the window. I screamed and she took off. It was *her,* Maisie was coming for me and Gabe, just like you said she would!'

'I didn't say that, exactly. Is Charles there with you?'

'Yes, we're all awake now.'

Dani wasn't surprised, the hysterical state that Kristin was in. 'Then make sure all the doors are locked and wait for me and DC Calder. We'll be there in half an hour.'

It was raining in sheets by the time they reached the

Riddells' property. Charles opened the front door as soon as Andy had switched off the engine. He'd obviously been watching for them to arrive.

He hustled the detectives through the door. 'I've given Kristin a brandy and settled Gabriel back down to sleep. Now we can go out and search for Maisie.'

Dani held up her hand. 'Wait a minute, Mr Riddell. We need to talk to your wife first, about what she saw.'

'But we can't waste any more time, surely?' He glanced behind them. 'And where are the Norwegian police? We need plenty of men on the ground to scour the area, it's absolutely vast.'

Andy placed a supportive hand on Charles' back, leading him gently but firmly towards the kitchen-diner, where Kristin was slumped on the sofa with a half full glass of spirits balanced precariously in her lap.

'Take a seat too, would you, Mr Riddell?' Dani turned towards Andy. 'Could you pour another brandy,' she asked him.

Charles seemed shell-shocked, but allowed himself to he shuffled into a chair opposite his wife and accepted the glass of brandy that was placed in his hand. Dani sat down next to the woman and said softly, 'what did you see, Kristin?'

She was trembling and her eyes were wide with fear. 'There was a figure pressed up to the glass. I saw the dark hair and her pale, expressionless face. It was Maisie.'

'What was this person wearing?' Dani asked.

Kristin shook her head. 'I don't know. It all happened so fast. As soon as she saw me, the girl ran away.'

'It's raining very hard out there. Don't you think that if Maisie were somewhere in the woods she'd take shelter in this weather? Why would she come to the house if she didn't want to be allowed in, or to see her father?'

'Because she wants to frighten me, that is why. Maisie wants me to think she'll harm Gabriel, she's torturing me!'

Charles looked confused. 'Why would she do that, Kristin? This doesn't make any sense.'

His wife snapped her head in his direction. 'Your precious daughter has always hated me. Don't say you haven't noticed.'

'It's been tough for Maisie, surely you understand that? She lost her family when I moved out here.'

'Plenty of children have divorced parents,' she muttered sourly.

'Perhaps you should tell your husband the truth, Kristin. I think it's time,' Dani said levelly.

'What does she mean?' Charles took a sip of the brandy, as if knowing that bad news was imminent.

'When I took the job at Barents Oil, I was a member of the Environmental Liberation Group. I was in a relationship with Andreas Nilsen and he wanted me to gather information for him.' Kristin allowed the words to settle between them.

Charles narrowed his eyes. 'Just what the hell are you admitting to?'

'I did provide Andreas with material in the first few months, but as I got to know you, I began stalling him. Then I fell in love with you, Charles. After that, I broke off all contact with the group. I've had nothing to do with them ever since.'

Charles turned shakily to look at Dani. 'What has this got to do with Maisie?'

'We believe that your daughter discovered Kristin's secret. Some letters that Maisie had written came into our possession and in them she discusses her suspicions about your wife.'

'Why didn't Maisie come straight to me with this?'

Andy took up the story. 'We think that Maisie was worried you wouldn't believe her. I suppose she felt that your new relationship was so strong it would be difficult to persuade you that Kristin had been disloyal.'

A flicker of recognition passed across the man's face, as if this possibility were entirely feasible. 'Why did she run away?'

'Our theory is that she was trying to reach Norway under her own steam, so that she could gather information against Kristin. She wanted to prove her case to you categorically.'

Charles leapt up out of his seat, spilling some of the brandy on the pure white carpet. 'Then that could very well have been my daughter outside tonight! What are we waiting for? Let's get out there and start looking!'

Andy stepped across and laid a hand on his shoulder once again, making Riddell immediately suspicious. 'There's something else, isn't there? Something you've not told us yet? For God's sake, Detective Chief Inspector, put me out of my misery!'

Chapter Forty Two

Dani waited until the man was sitting back in his seat before she carried on. 'We were going to come and see you this morning anyway, before I got Kristin's phone call. We received a piece of fresh evidence late last night.' Bevan's tone became grave. 'Two of my team have been checking out the possible sighting of Maisie at the docks in Newcastle on the evening after she went missing. They decided to expand their investigation to include all of the ports within thirty miles of the Tyne. In a town called Blyth, they gained new information. A fishing boat, with a crew of three men on board, set out late on that Thursday evening. As far as anyone can tell, it never came back.'

Charles gasped. 'They can't know for sure that Maisie and these others were on board, or even what happened to the boat.'

'The skipper of the fishing trawler had no family to speak of and his absence wasn't noticed. One of his crew, however, a young man called Davy Webb, was reported missing on Friday 20th March. My officers spoke with his parents. They claimed that the skipper was involved in numerous criminal activities and they'd been trying to persuade their son to end his involvement with the man. Webb's parents suggested that the other crew member was working illegally, and this was the reason he was able to disappear without trace. These men appear to be just the kind of operators who would agree to accept money to transport illegal immigrants to the continent.'

'What if the crew reached some European port and simply haven't returned back home yet?' Charles' voice was desperate.

Dani slid forward in her seat. 'There was a terrible storm on the night of the nineteenth. Even the big container ships had to return to port. The skipper of the trawler took a huge risk by setting sail in that weather. I suppose the money persuaded him it was a good idea.'

Riddell looked stricken.

'We've checked every European port reachable from Blyth. None had recorded the arrival of a fishing trawler that night, or in the days that followed. I'm very sorry, Mr Riddell. It seems as if Maisie never survived the voyage.'

The man's body began to heave with sobs. 'Has Fiona been told yet?'

'A senior officer will be paying your ex-wife a visit first thing in the morning. Let's give her a few more hours of peace first.'

Kristin cast her eyes about the room wildly. 'What about the girl I saw at the window? How do you explain that?'

Dani put her hand on the woman's arm. 'It's been a very stressful few days for all of us. It isn't surprising that sometimes our minds might play tricks. I should never have suggested that Maisie could be in the area, trying to persecute you. All it did was to upset you even further. We've found no evidence of Maisie's presence since we've been back here in Stavanger. We jumped the gun.'

The detectives stood up. 'We'll leave you alone now. Please try to get some sleep.'

Charles slammed his heavy glass onto a side table. 'Could you take Kristin with you? Give her a lift to her mother's place, it's not far. Gabriel is sleeping and I don't wish to disturb him. I'll drop the boy off there in the morning.'

*

The sun was rising in a blaze of orange as they returned to their hotel. Dani wondered if there was any point in going back to bed. Andy must have been thinking the same thing because he nodded towards a bakery opposite, where a man in a crisp, white apron was just pulling up the shutters.

'Do you fancy a coffee?'

'Absolutely,' she replied with a thin smile.

Within a few minutes, the bakery and café was milling with people, most of them on their way to work. Dani felt the kind of emptiness in her stomach that you only get after being up half the night, and when the last thing you actually want is food.

'Alice and Dan did a great job,' Andy said graciously, setting two steaming mugs on the table.

'I suspect that DC Mann was the brains behind the operation. I must commend her actions to the DCS.'

'Who is going to inform Fiona Riddell?'

'I really regret not being able to pass on the news to the poor woman myself. I've requested that DS Rose do it. But I also called Phil last night and asked if he could be there too. I think Fiona's going to need him over the next few months.'

'What about Jane?' Andy asked cautiously, taking a warming sip of his coffee.

'To hell with Jane,' Dani said unguardedly. 'It's bloody obvious she doesn't need Phil at all. Only to make the packed lunches and provide childcare.'

Andy nodded, thinking he was in total agreement. 'Have we failed, Ma'am?' he added unexpectedly.

'There was never anything we could have done. Maisie was dead within thirty six hours of her going missing. She'd told absolutely no one of her plans. If she'd confided in just one friend, we might have been able to save her.'

'Well, it looks like she's succeeded in breaking up her dad's new marriage, even if Maisie never got to witness it.'

'Charles is simply overwhelmed with grief. It will take a long while before he can even contemplate what Kristin has done. I'm sure he'll forgive her in the end. They've got Gabriel to think of now.'

Andy said nothing, he wasn't so sure. He knew a little something about male pride. A powerful man like Charles Riddell wouldn't like having been deceived for all that time.

'When we get back to our rooms, I'll call the airport and organise a flight home.' Dani drained her cup.

'Look, Ma'am. It seems a bit silly for you not to see Dieter whilst we're here in Stavanger. I know I've not exactly been approving, but if you want to book a later flight. I wouldn't mind.'

Dani felt as if she could lean over the table and kiss him, her chest beginning to flutter with excitement. 'Thanks Andy. I really would like to drop in on him before we go. I'm not sure when we'll get another chance like this.'

Chapter Forty Three

Dani went back to the guesthouse to change her clothes before she headed out to the Bureau. She applied her make-up carefully, trying to mask the fact she'd had almost no sleep. After the sad news they'd received regarding Maisie, Bevan felt guilty about experiencing so much excitement at the thought of seeing Dieter again. But she rationalised it by telling herself that these were the natural emotions one felt when in the early stages of such an all-consuming relationship – when the bond between two people was so immediate and strong.

She left Andy in the old town and took the hire car to the police headquarters on the outskirts of Stavanger. Dani assumed that Dieter would have returned to work by now, as he'd been so worried about leaving Magda with too much on her plate.

Detective Hustad was standing by her desk as Dani stepped off the escalator. The woman gave her a warm smile. 'I'm pleased to see you again.'

Dani's expression became sombre and she took hold of Magda's hands.

'There is bad news, about the girl?'

Bevan nodded.

Magda sighed. 'There was always going to be, after she was missing for so long. Our training teaches us this. But it doesn't make it any easier to hear.'

'No, it doesn't.'

'Have you told Karlsen yet?'

'I've not had the opportunity, is he here?' Dani glanced about the office floor, trying not to sound too eager.

'He is out at Byfjorden, meeting one of his contacts.'

The disappointment in Bevan's face must have been obvious. 'I've got to catch a flight at lunchtime.'

'Why don't you go and find him there? It's not far. I'll give you the directions. The fjord is very beautiful, especially on a clear day such as this. You should see it before returning home.' She smiled. 'I'm very relieved to have Dieter back at work. The Inspector from Oslo has finally gone. If he'd had a few more days to dig around, he might have made life difficult for us. Dieter isn't very good at paperwork.'

*

Dani kept glancing at the clock on the dashboard, as she drove towards the Byfjorden. Apparently, there was a car park at a viewing platform where Dieter usually made contact with his informants. Magda had drawn her a sketchy map. The journey was quite stunning. It was a clear, sunny day and the mountains were like nothing Dani had ever seen. They were somehow on a larger scale than those of her native Scotland and the occasional simple Nordic cabin populated the green hillsides.

A German car with dark paintwork pulled out of the turning as Dani arrived at the beauty spot. She allowed it to leave before proceeding onto the bumpy track that led to the viewing platform. She was immensely relieved to see that Dieter's car was still there. Bevan parked up next to it but noticed the detective was not inside. Dani got out and walked towards the platform, which was boarded with strips of solid pine and had railings made out of the same wood, to protect visitors from the height of the drop down to the fjord below.

Dieter was leaning against the barrier, looking out towards the most glorious view Bevan had ever seen. Mountains encircled them and the sun was at its highest point in the cloudless blue sky.

She touched him gently on the arm, her heart beating so fast she thought it might explode.

He turned very slowly. When she caught sight of his face the expression he wore chilled her to the bone. '*Dani*? What are you doing here?'

'There were developments in the Maisie Riddell case. Andy and I came back to pursue them. But it's all over now. I'm going home in an hour. It just seemed like madness not to try and see you.'

Dieter appeared to have composed himself. He leant down and kissed her tenderly. 'I'm sorry darling, I just didn't expect to see you in Norway. You took me by surprise.'

Dani put up a hand to touch his cheek. 'I apologise for not coming to the airport with you the other day,' her voice was full of remorse. 'My friend is recovering well now,' she added, as if the man had actually enquired.

'It doesn't matter. You're here with me now.' He swept her into an embrace. They gripped each other tightly.

Dani felt all her doubts and worries disappear. She looked over Dieter's shoulder at the shimmering water so far below them, pulling him closer and whispering the sweet reassurances of the devoted lover into his ear.

'I've really got to go,' she said finally. 'The flight leaves in half an hour. Andy will be waiting.'

'I'll follow you in the car, so we can say goodbye at the airport.'

Dani hesitated for a moment. 'There was just one thing I wanted to ask you about.'

Dieter stood very still, his face a total blank. 'Of

course, what is it?'

'Andy and I went to the university. We spoke with a professor there. He was convinced that the attack on Aron Holm was a deliberate attempt to prevent his work from continuing.' Dani touched the collar of Dieter's padded jacket. 'Was it really you who attacked Holm? Or are you protecting somebody? My investigative instincts tell me that the assault can't simply have been an isolated incident, or a case of mistaken identity. Coincidences like that just don't happen in real life.'

Dieter took a step backwards. 'Are you still investigating the Aron Holm assault? You told me you'd let it go.'

'Yes, I have. But Andy still had doubts, and I couldn't stop him from asking questions or it would have looked suspicious.'

'It sounds like you are the one with doubts.'

Dani didn't like the expression on the man's face.

'I'm a police officer, Dieter. It's my job to question everything.'

'Well, I really wished you hadn't.' The man looked genuinely disappointed.

Dani didn't know what to say to this. She turned to walk towards the hire car, knowing that she was running the risk of missing her flight. There just wasn't time to continue with the discussion right now. Dieter shot his arm out and twisted her back round. 'Where are you going? We're not finished here yet.'

'I need to get to the airport. I shouldn't have come.'

The detective kept hold of her arm. 'I really like you Dani. I'm sorry it's ended in this way.'

Bevan tried to wriggle herself free of his grasp. 'What are you talking about? – are you calling things off just because I asked you about Aron Holm?'

Dieter began dragging her towards the thin wooden barrier, where the view across to the mountains was breath-taking. 'I don't think you're ever going to let it go. When we were back in Glasgow it seemed as if you would.'

Dani's mind was ticking over fast, she managed to dig her heavy soled boot into a gap between the boards and anchor herself for a moment. 'Are you so very frightened of facing that assault charge, Dieter? Or is there something more?'

'Those people who you saw driving away?'

She nodded.

'They are very powerful and influential in this city. They simply cannot allow Aron Holm to destroy the economy. Many lives depend upon the oil industry. Not just here, but also in your own homeland.'

'Did they pay you to attack him?'

'That isn't relevant. I agreed with their arguments. The man had to be stopped.'

Dani was thinking quickly. 'So you knew that Aron Holm would be returning to his car alone, because Jakob was going home that evening with *your* wife. Was Sofie in on the plan too?'

The man's face flashed red with rage. 'Leave her out of this! She knows nothing.'

In that moment, Dani could see that Dieter still loved her and had probably never stopped. She rammed her other boot down hard on his ankle, causing him to yelp with pain and briefly relax his grip. Bevan shook him off and made a run for the car, desperately searching through her bag for the keys.

She wasn't fast enough. Dieter caught her around the waist and they both fell forward, with Dani hitting her head against the car bonnet. She was momentarily dazed. It gave Dieter time to haul her back onto the platform and shove her against the wooden railing.

'Getting rid of me isn't going to help,' she gasped. 'The Chief of Police is on to you, it's just a matter of time before somebody starts digging into your old cases again – I wonder what else those people paid you to do? And how about Magda? I don't believe she'd turn a blind eye to murder.'

Dieter slapped her across the face. 'Be quiet. You are the only one who found out the truth about the Aron Holm assault. Luckily for me, you haven't reported it yet.' The man sighed and looked out at the landscape. 'The beauty of the fjords is that they are so vast and deep. You will rest peacefully here, I promise.'

The Norwegian possessed all the advantages in terms of height and weight. He could lift Bevan up easily. She tried desperately to hook her leg around one of the barrier's supports, but the smooth wood was difficult to gain a purchase on. Dani thought about her father and how he was going to be left quite alone in the world. This made her experience a surge of anger and she managed to send out a fierce kick which caught Dieter in the ribs. He stumbled backwards and Dani collapsed onto the barrier, her legs swinging outwards over the drop, but securing an arm firmly around the top, trying not to allow her gaze to turn to what lay many metres below.

As Dieter made to stand up, his legs were cut out from under him. Bevan could see Andy Calder wielding the spiky tree branch which he'd used to bring the Norwegian to the ground.

'Quick!' Dani called out to her colleague. 'I can't hold on much longer!'

Andy dropped to his knees and attached cuffs to Dieter's hands, dragging him towards another figure, standing further away, by the parked cars. He ran towards his boss at full pelt, throwing his arms over the side and hoisting her back across the barrier. Dani fell onto the platform with a thud, her limbs aching like hell.

Chapter Forty Four

They weren't able to board a flight back to Glasgow for many hours. Dani was taken away by ambulance from the banks of the Byfjorden and had been treated at Stavanger hospital for most of the afternoon, where she was questioned by police officers who had come straight from Oslo.

In fact, the DCI only saw Andy again when she walked stiffly down the aisle of the aircraft and lowered herself into the seat next to him. In a rare gesture of affection from the DC, he placed an arm around her and she rested her weary head against his shoulder.

'I see you're wearing the jumper,' she said quietly.

'Just for you, Ma'am. I thought you might need cheering up.'

She managed a smile. 'How did you know we were at the fjord?'

'After you left the guesthouse, I decided not to waste the morning. I was curious about what Professor Holgren said to us at the university, so I decided to have another talk with Andreas Nilsen. I found him much more amenable on this occasion. I spoke to him about Holgren's suggestion that there were police officers in the employ of oil executives. Andreas told me that he suspected Dieter Karlsen was one of those corrupt officers. That was why Nilsen was so obstructive when we came to his house with Dieter in tow. When I found this out, I knew I had to warn you before you got in too deep with the guy. I showed up at the police headquarters and Magda told me you'd gone out to meet him. I persuaded her to drive me to the beauty spot as quickly as possible. I think it came as a terrible shock when she saw what Dieter was up to when we got there.'

'Thank you, Andy. You saved my life.' She straightened up and looked him in the eye. 'I withheld information from you, about the Aron Holm assault. Sofie Karlsen told me that her husband was the one who attacked Holm. She said he'd mistaken him for her lover. Dieter begged me to keep quiet about it and I did. I think that's the real reason he came to Glasgow. I've been a fool.'

'You weren't the only one who kept quiet about it. Magda suspected something too but never said anything because she trusted Dieter. She told me all about it on the way back into town this afternoon. But Magda never knew he was on the take.'

'Do you think he really did those things for the money? Maybe he agreed with the principles of the people paying him. If Holm creates a future without oil, thousands will lose their jobs.'

'It's always about the money, Dani, you know that.'

The DCI sat back and clipped on her belt, listening to the engines fire up as the plane lifted them high over the town. She glanced out of the small window and could observe, from this vantage point, just how closely connected the country was to the dark, restless sea.

*

'It's a shame you didn't get a chance to see Detective Sharpe again before he went back to the United States,' Bill said wistfully, as his wife re-entered the living room with their coffees.

'It was very fortunate that Sam responded to your phone call. Things could have worked out quite differently if he hadn't,' Dani replied with feeling, taking a cup from the tray.

'Goodness,' said Joy, 'we owe that man a great deal.'

Bill was sitting in a chair opposite their guest. His arm was still bandaged and supported by a sling. 'He promised to return for the trial. This time we're certain to get a conviction.' Bill had a determined expression on his face.

'Do the police know why Erskine focussed on Sinclair and Anton in particular?'

'Apparently, Erskine had been spending most of his time tracking down individuals responsible for the sexual exploitation of underage girls. His computer hard drive revealed that he'd tapped into some websites that cater for these types of men. They operate just on the fringes of legality, so I'm told. Erskine heard about the Fisherman's Bar through one of the sites and later, Clive Anton's club on London Road. He staked out both of these establishments for weeks. Erskine gained a good knowledge of which men were running the brothels. He followed the key players for a while and noted their habits.'

'And because you were hanging around the Fisherman's Bar and having in-depth discussions with the landlady, he thought you were one of the men in charge.' Dani sipped her coffee.

'After that first Friday evening I spent there, Erskine watched our house overnight. But he knew I'd spotted him, so he didn't return for a few days. Then he saw me again at the bar and this time I went upstairs, coming out not long after with one of the girls. Perhaps he thought I was moving her to another establishment. I think that spurred him on to strike.'

'But he didn't know that Sam was staying at the

house with you?' Dani put in.

'No, that was his mistake. Erskine thought Joy wouldn't be back for an hour and he'd have plenty of time to slit my throat and change his clothing before he left. I'm far older than his previous victims. He must have thought it would be relatively straightforward on this occasion.'

'I suppose he *was* targeting people who were doing the most terrible things - apart from you, dear,' Joy said thoughtfully. 'Erskine has actually saved a lot of girls from an awful fate.'

Bill wriggled up in his seat. 'Detective Sharpe said that Erskine's motive wasn't so honourable. He suggested that the man had simply developed a taste for murder. The fact that he selected victims involved in the sex trade was purely for the purpose of self-justification.'

'I think Sam was quite correct. Erskine didn't have the right to set himself up as judge and executioner, nor did he have the resources of the police. He was bound to end up attacking an innocent man which eventually, he did,' Dani added.

'Let's just hope that the jury doesn't feel sympathy for Erskine, like they did the last time. I expect there'll be plenty of people in the country who will.' Bill looked philosophical.

'There are never any guarantees,' Dani muttered quietly.

'It's very sad, about your young girl, Maisie,' Joy said tentatively, changing the subject.

'Yes, it is. There will be a memorial service next week at the Cathedral.'

'Oh, we'd like to come,' Joy said quickly.

'I think there will be lots of folk there, you'd be very welcome I'm sure.'

'It's so difficult for the parents when there isn't a body to bury. It really denies them closure. That was something we at least had with Neil. You are always clinging to a kind of hope otherwise.'

'I don't think Maisie's parents are clinging to any false hopes,' Dani explained patiently, 'they are both suffering from devastating grief.'

'We know all about that,' Bill said resignedly.

The three friends sat in companionable silence, each of them thinking about poor Maisie Riddell.

It was Joy who intruded on their thoughts. 'We read that you uncovered an incidence of police corruption whilst you were in Norway. So some good has come out of all this.'

Dani's heart skipped a beat. She sincerely hoped that her emotions were not showing on her face. 'Yes, a man called Detective Karlsen was taking bribes to do the bidding of a group of local business people.'

'The papers made it sound as if he was in the pocket of one of the big oil corporations over there,' Bill said with interest.

'Actually, it had nothing to do with the major oil companies in the end. The men who were paying Karlsen were simply crooks. They made their money out of buying and selling in oil shares and were prepared to do whatever it took to protect their investments. The Chief of Police already had his suspicions about Dieter. They'd been watching him for some time. Andy and I just brought things to a head with our investigations.'

'Did you know this corrupt policeman quite well then,' Joy asked innocently.

'I got to know him reasonably well, yes. Actually, I came to like him, although Andy never did.'

'That's funny,' Bill said. 'It's usually you who has the good instincts about people.'

Chapter Forty Five

Returning to the flat was hard. Dani had spent most of the day holed up with DCS Nicholson and Phil Boag, discussing the latter's future in the police force. Nicholson knew what a talented officer Phil was, he'd worked with him for many years. The DCS seemed convinced that Dani's DS was going through some kind of mid-life crisis. Phil kept quiet throughout much of the debate, which appeared to confirm Nicholson's theory of a breakdown.

In the end, they decided upon a phased return to work and the instigation of three months of intensive therapy, to be paid for by the division. Phil wouldn't be losing his rank. For this, Dani was hugely grateful. She couldn't have borne having to say goodbye to such a good colleague and friend, on top of everything else.

She pushed the front door open tentatively, as if expecting a menacing figure to be lurking inside. Instead, it was as quiet and still as the grave, which, of course, was what she was dreading most. Dani had always been someone who enjoyed living alone. She worked long hours and valued the peace and seclusion that her home provided. The idea Dieter might have taken this away from her really hurt. But she supposed it was her own fault, for letting the man in here.

Dani deposited her coat and bag and strode into the kitchen, throwing on every light switch to inject some cheer. She knew that with time she'd get over it. Her sense of peace and contentment would return. Perhaps a week or two on Colonsay with her father would help to speed up the process. Dani smiled at the thought of this. As she opened a cupboard to fix herself some food, the smile died on her lips. She was confronted by shelves filled with the stuff Dieter had bought for her. There were packets of flour and baking products, jars of interesting jams and pickles. The types of goods she would never have sought out for herself.

The DCI had been holding back the emotions she felt for days, but now the tears fell. She sat at the table with her head in her hands. The anguish lasted for about half an hour and then it stopped, as abruptly as it had begun. Dani lifted her head and found she was feeling hungry.

As she made a move back towards the kitchen, the doorbell rang. Dani dabbed at her face with a tissue and walked carefully along the corridor. She opened up to find Andy standing on the step, cradling a bottle of wine. Behind him was Carol, holding onto the handles of Amy's pink pram.

Dani beamed with genuine pleasure and stood back to allow them to enter. Within minutes, the flat was filled with noise and laughter. Bevan brought down some glasses and fixed them all a drink. She checked out one of the lower cupboards and discovered packets of gourmet crisps and nuts, which she shook out into bowls. There was even fresh orange juice in the fridge for Amy.

'Were you expecting visitors?' Andy asked in surprise, not used to his boss's kitchen being quite so well stocked.

'No, I just like to have a few things in, just in case.'

Carol wanted to know all about Norway and they chatted for as long as Amy was prepared to play quietly with the dolls she had brought with her.

Dani glanced down at the little girl, with her

golden curls and contented expression. 'I should really get some toys in for Amy to play with when you come over again,' she said distractedly.

Andy nearly choked on his Merlot. 'Dani Bevan shopping in Mothercare! I'd pay good money to see that one!'

Dani turned to her colleague and laughed good-naturedly, leaning over to pour more wine into their glasses.

'Come on, Andy, I'm sure Dani buys a lot of things for her friends' children.' Not for the first time Carol was worried her husband may have overstepped the mark.

'You wouldn't be so keen to leap to Dani's defence if you knew what she said about the jumpers you bought me for Christmas,' Andy retorted with a wink.

Dani stood with her mouth open, entirely lost for words, until Carol started to giggle. Amy looked up at her mum and started to laugh too and soon they were all in a fit of hysterics, with nobody being quite sure what had set them off in the first place.

*

Chapter Forty Six

After several days of interminably wet weather, the skies over Stavanger had begun to clear. Charles Riddell was tidying up the toys in his son's bedroom. For the time being, Gabriel was at his grandmother's house with Kristin but soon they would start the process of deciding upon access arrangements and other such technicalities. About which, he actually had a great deal of knowledge, having gone through the whole thing five years before.

Charles knew that the collapse of a second marriage was a badge of personal failure. No longer could one blame the poor decisions and inexperience of youth. But he was quite sure that Kristin's deception was something he could not forgive. The knowledge that half the city was aware of her involvement with this environmental group was more than his pride could bear. Even if that wasn't true, he'd always suspect it.

The house would be sold and the profits split between them. Kristin would be well taken care of. Charles was happy for his wife to have custody of Gabriel. As long as he retained his visitation rights, which he was sure wouldn't be a problem.

Charles padded around the vast kitchen-diner. What had once been a dream home for him and his young family, now felt cold and empty, the fixtures and fittings seemed stark and minimalist, which was a look that had never previously been his style. It was amazing how living within a new culture could so quickly and subtly change your tastes and habits.

The sun was now strong enough for Charles to

turn the lock on the large patio doors and slide them open to let in the spring-like air. He could smell the pine trees, their natural scent stimulated by the continuous rain of the previous week. He walked back towards the kitchen stove, filling a kettle with water and placing it on the light. He sensed a shadow falling onto the work top in front of him and decided the clouds must have blown over once more. Thinking he'd need to pull the door shut again, he turned around.

A figure was standing perfectly still on the garden patio, although he'd heard no one approach. At first, Charles thought he was dreaming; that the trauma of the past few weeks had sent him quite mad. He decided to enjoy the vision, to revel in it. He stared at her silky black hair and rejoiced in the paleness of her skin and those watery green eyes. When the vision broke into a smile and walked towards him he thought his legs might buckle. It was she who held him strongly and kept the man upright. Once his daughter was in his arms, Charles knew for certain she was real and he let out a cry of pure joy.

Charles insisted that Maisie have a bath. He selected some of Kristin's jogging pants and a sweatshirt and they seemed to fit her rather well. Charles made them both a hot chocolate and lit the wood-burning stove. He sat next to her on the sofa and held her hand. 'Please tell me where you've been. We thought you were dead.'

Maisie touched her father's face. 'Of course I'll tell you. I never expected to be hiding for so long.'

'I want to know everything, right from when you were back home in Glasgow.'

Maisie sighed. 'I wasn't getting on well with Mum. Now I've had time to think I can see her side of it more. But back then I was desperate to get away. I went to a club in the city one night and got talking to this guy. He was a DJ and I told him I wanted to sing professionally. He asked me to perform for him and he was really impressed. Ray set up some gigs where I could do the backing vocals. I didn't get paid at first, but later on, one of the bands needed a lead singer and Ray recommended me. After that, I started earning decent money.'

Charles tried hard not to show his anger. 'How come your mother allowed you to go out and do all this?'

'She didn't know, Dad. I slipped out of the house after Mum was in bed, or sometimes I got friends to say I was at a sleepover with them.'

Her father nodded, he was trying desperately to understand.

'Some of the men in those clubs were really sleazy, but Ray was actually an okay bloke. I pretended to be with him and that kept the creeps at bay. By the start of this year, I'd saved a few hundred quid.'

'I would have given you that money if you'd asked, Maisie.'

'I'm aware of that, Dad. But, I enjoyed the gigs and it's good to earn your own cash. It made me independent of Mum. I could buy clothes and stuff without running it by her.'

Charles could appreciate that concept. He'd been earning his own money since he was a teenager and worked his way through university.

'I don't think I had any sort of clear idea about what I was going to do with it, there was no plan. I was just enjoying the freedom it gave me.' She looked sheepish. 'On Wednesday afternoons, when we had this dickhead of a teacher for activities who never took the register, I used to walk out of the school gates and get a bus into town. I would go to the shops, have a coffee, whatever I liked. But one day, it turned a bit sour. I saw Mum with this guy. I knew she'd been seeing somebody because she was being all secretive about text messages and stuff. Then she went to a really posh hairdressers in town and got a proper, expensive style. It was pretty obvious she had a new boyfriend. But what I didn't know was that Mum was seeing Georgie's dad – the married father of my *best friend*.'

'Your mother is entitled to a private life,' Charles ventured, realising that to say otherwise would make him a hypocrite.

'I think I can understand that now. But I was really angry back then. When I saw them together it was the last straw. I knew I didn't want to live with Mum anymore.'

'Why didn't you come straight to *me*,' he implored.

'Come on, you know that Kristin and I don't like each other. That was another part of the issue, actually. I found out about Kristin being a member of an ecological group. I thought she'd only married you to get information about your company. I really hated her then and sort of wanted to split you both up.'

'Kristin has moved out. We're going to get a divorce.'

'I figured that out when I saw her and Gabriel leaving with their suitcases and bags the other day.'

'Have you been watching the house?'

Maisie nodded. 'Yeah, sorry.'

Realisation seemed to dawn on Charles. 'So Kristin *did* see you at Gabriel's window. She didn't imagine it.'

'That's right. Can I explain everything from the beginning, Dad? I think it might make more sense that way.'

Charles felt dizzy with confusion but he allowed her to continue.

'It only took a few days to organise my trip. I'd heard rumours about some guys at the clubs who brought girls into the country who were illegal, so they could work cheaply behind the bar and in the kitchens. I knew they got taken to other places too, like Amsterdam and Stockholm. I thought that with enough money, I'd be able to get myself here to Norway. Then I could gather evidence against Kristin and blow her secret sky high.'

'You could have just told me, sweetheart.'

Maisie raised her eyebrows. 'Come on, you were infatuated with her. When we were all together in a room, you didn't look at anyone but Kristin.'

Charles was silenced by this, but he could accept that she was probably right. Up until his daughter's disappearance that was, when Kristin's spell had been well and truly broken.

'It turned out that I didn't actually need all that much money to get myself smuggled out of the country, just a few hundred pounds. I'd arranged to meet these two guys at junction 20 of the M8. I left school and walked to the rendezvous point. I didn't want to get spotted travelling on a bus. When I arrived, the two men had a van. It was quite big and there were other people in the back, men and women, a few of them were really young. They looked scared and I felt bad for them. We had to squeeze in really tightly and the journey was uncomfortable. They were taking us down to Newcastle, which is where the men said I'd be getting on a boat.'

'The police traced you there. Somebody on the docks recognised you from your missing posters.'

'The two men kept arguing, not always in English either, so I didn't really know what was going on. They made us sleep the night in the back of the van.

I think the boat they were expecting hadn't docked yet. It was bloody uncomfortable and I was really starting to regret the whole thing. The following day, they kept us in the van until it started to get dark, then the guys marched us around the port, trying to get someone to smuggle us onto a ship. I realised then that their plan must have gone wrong. The boat they'd been expecting hadn't turned up. I'd not paid them the rest of the money yet so I made a decision. I saw the huge ferry port and reckoned I'd have better luck trying to sneak on board one of those ships than staying with the group. I was much less conspicuous than them, if you know what I mean. We parted ways at the docks, with no hard feelings.'

Charles leant forward. 'The group you were with travelled up the coast to Blyth, they found a fisherman willing to take them across the sea in his trawler. But there was a terrible storm. The boat was lost and they were all drowned.'

Maisie put a hand up to her mouth. 'Oh my God! Those poor people! There were girls in the gang who were younger than me.' She began to cry.

'The police have started the task of trying to find out who was on board, other than the crew. They believed you were one of them. The rest were illegal immigrants, about to be deported from Britain. I expect they'll be able to put names to them in the end.'

'It's so unfair,' she sobbed. 'They were totally harmless.'

'So, how did you eventually get here?' he prompted, when she'd recovered her composure sufficiently.

'I headed up towards the ferry terminal. I noticed that some of the ships were travelling to Kristiansand. I hung around the waiting room for a while and this group of student types came in.

They'd been in the pub and were really jolly. I think they were actually stoned. I joined them and pretended I was a student from Glasgow University. They were going on a back-packing trip for the Easter break. When it was time for the ferry to board, I put my arm around one of the guys and kind of blended into the crowd. The steward looked at all the tickets, which were attached in a long strip, but it was cursory really. I don't think they pay much attention on these overnight ferries.'

Charles thought she was probably right. 'Did you stay with the students?'

'Yeah, I sat with them for the voyage,' her face became grave. 'Dad, it was awful. It rained the whole way and the ship was tossed about by the waves. We were all being sick into the litter bins. It wasn't at all like going to Arran. I'm *never* taking that route again.'

Her father couldn't help but smile.

'It was mid-morning when we docked. I was so relieved to be back on dry land. I strolled off the boat with my student friends and there were no problems at Customs. I reckon that if you're female, white and middle class, you can probably move about the world as freely as you choose.'

Charles thought this was an exaggeration, but he could certainly see her point.

'The students were going to Oslo, so I tagged along. We took a coach and this time I had a proper ticket. When we reached the capital, I parted ways with them. They're probably still back-packing round Europe somewhere, permanently stoned.'

'Which is why they never realised the police were looking for you.'

Maisie shrugged her shoulders. 'I don't think they'd have ratted on me even if they had. Anyway, while I was in Oslo, I bought a load of outdoor equipment, like a sleeping bag, a proper rucksack and really warm clothes. I thought the local police might be looking for me so I hitch-hiked to the outskirts of Stavanger.'

Charles looked shocked.

'Despite all the Scandi-noir on T.V, I know that Norway is a really safe and friendly place. Besides, I had a plan. I headed towards the forest. I remembered the old cabin we used to walk to, before you and Kristin bought this place, when I came on holiday to Norway and it was just the two of us, do you remember?'

Charles nodded. 'It's about two miles from here. The place is practically derelict. Don't tell me you've been staying in there?'

'It's only really been a few days. I fixed the cabin up a bit and made it as watertight as I could. It's right in the heart of the forest. I've been really well protected from the rain. My plan was to try and gather some evidence on Kristin. I went into town a few times when I first arrived and hung about the university, but I didn't know where to start, especially without my laptop. So I changed my strategy a bit.' Maisie looked guilty. 'Dad, I've got a confession to make.'

'Go ahead.' He didn't have the energy to look stern.

'I decided to make her life a misery instead. I wanted to freak her out, I suppose.' She took a deep breath. 'It was me who moved Gabriel's pram.'

'What?'

'I'd been watching the house and saw that Kristin had left him outside. I didn't want to hurt him, just scare her a bit, so I ran over and wheeled him into the trees. He didn't wake up and I was always close by. I certainly didn't expect her to call the police. It took them *ages* to find him. Bloody idiots.'

'Maisie, that was a very cruel thing to do. Kristin was beside herself.'

'I know. But she didn't care that *I'd* been pushed out of the family. I wanted her to know what it felt like to lose someone you love. I realise it was wrong now. I'm genuinely sorry.'

'What made you turn up at the house today?'

'I knew you were here on your own. I've been keeping an eye on things. I saw Kristin and Gabriel leave. I just needed to pluck up the courage to face you.'

'I've been praying day and night for you to come home. I'd hardly have been angry with you.'

'But I've caused so many problems and I upset Kristin. I thought I'd be in trouble.'

Charles cupped his daughter's face in his hands. 'Of course not, to have you here with me is a miracle. We must tell your mother, we can't let her go on suffering.'

'Being in the cabin has given me time to think. I still don't feel I can live with her, but I realise that Mum was only doing her best.'

'Good, because she loves you very much, you mustn't ever doubt that. Now, I've been doing some thinking myself. I'm going to move back to Scotland. It will have to be Aberdeen I'm afraid, because that's the only place I'll get work. You can come and live with me. We'll find you a good school nearby.'

'What about Gabriel?' Maisie looked concerned.

'I'll see him regularly. The flight from Aberdeen to Stavanger is very short.'

'I don't want you to do that. He's just a baby. I can't be responsible for taking his dad away from him. I've been watching the little guy during the time I've been in the cabin. He's really sweet. I want to get to know him better.'

Charles was puzzled. 'What are you suggesting?'

'We can stay here. I can go to a local school. I like it in Norway, I feel happy here and I want to get to know my little brother. I don't want to leave the forest.'

'I'm sure that desire will change, but for now it would make sense. I don't want to live apart from you *or* Gabriel. But what about your mother? We can't abandon her completely.'

Maisie smiled. 'She's got Phil to look after her. Having some time on their own to get to know each other better would do them both good.'

'I thought you were worried about Georgie Boag?'

'It's not like her dad will be going anywhere and when I thought about Phil, while I was in my cabin, I remembered how sad he always seemed, at home in that big house by himself. Mrs Boag doesn't need anyone else. The school is all that matters to her. Georgie can have two mums.'

Charles nodded and patted Maisie on the knee. 'That's enough talk for now. Let me make you up a bed for the night. I want to be allowed to look after you for a while, before the outside world descends upon us.' He stood up.

'I'd love that, but before I go to bed, can I use the phone? I'd really like to ring Mum.'

*

To find out more about my books and to read articles and reviews please visit my blog, The RetroReview at:

www.wordpress.KatherinePathak.com

For special offers and news of new releases follow me on Twitter:

@KatherinePathak

If you would like to discuss the novel with me, use the hashtag #OnADarkSea

If you enjoyed this book, please take a moment to write me a brief review. Reviews really help to introduce new readers to my books and this allows me to keep on writing.

Many Thanks

Katherine.

Thanks for reading!

Made in the USA
San Bernardino, CA
27 May 2016